3

THE LONG SEARCH

THE LONG SEARCH

by Christine Pullein-Thompson

Bradbury Press / New York
Maxwell Macmillan Canada / Toronto
Maxwell Macmillan International
New York / Oxford / Singapore / Sydney

First U.S. edition 1993

Bradbury Press
Macmillan Publishing Company
866 Third Avenue
New York, NY 10022

Maxwell Macmillan Canada, Inc.
1200 Eglinton Avenue East
Suite 200
Don Mills, Ontario M3C 3N1

Macmillan Publishing Company is part of the
Maxwell Communication Group of Companies.

First published 1991 by Andersen Press, London
Printed and bound in the United States of America
10 9 8 7 6 5 4 3 2 1

The text of this book is set in 13-point Melior.

Library of Congress Cataloging-in-Publication Data
Pullein-Thompson, Christine.
The long search / by Christine Pullein-Thompson.—1st U.S. ed.
p. cm.
Summary: At the request of his gravely ill grandmother, twelve-
year-old Ion Radu sets out to find his parents who had been
taken as political prisoners years before, and he is caught up
in the 1989 revolution in Romania.
ISBN 0-02-775445-6
1. Romania—History—Revolution, 1989—Juvenile fiction.
[1. Romania—History—Revolution, 1989—Fiction.] I. Title.
PZ7.P959Lo   1993
[Fic]—dc20   92-40349

Contents

THE LONG SEARCH

1

"I'm Going to Find My Parents"

ION WISHED NOW that he had gone with his uncle and his family to England. He had gone part of the way and then returned to look after his grandmother, and now she was dying. How long it would take, no one knew. There was no doctor in the village. No medicines. Neighbors appeared with thin soup for her to drink and herbal medicines for her to take. But she wasn't getting better. Maria, who lived alone, came in to wash her every day. She sighed and shook her head. "If only she could get to a hospital," she said. "But even if we got her there, the hospital wouldn't take her in. They don't accept old ladies of seventy anymore. Not unless you bribe the doctor, and you haven't enough money for that, Ion."

So Ion milked the cow as usual and brought in the geese. Another day or two and the geese would be kept inside for the winter. There was hay enough for the one cow they had left. But the cellar below the house, where they stored their food, was almost empty.

Ion wanted someone else to come and take over. He had done his best. He did not know what more he could do for his grandmother. He was afraid that if she died, the local officials would take him to an orphanage and later force him to become a secret policeman. The very thought of it made his stomach churn. If only I had gone with Uncle Fanel to England, I would have been all right, he thought.

He took the milk to the cellar and strained it there. He took half a cupful to his grandmother and gave it to her. "It's fresh from the cow," he said. It was what she had said to him when he was small, as though being fresh from the cow gave it a magic that older milk did not possess. Ion did not believe in such magic anymore.

His grandmother drank it slowly, spluttering between sips. Maria had put a poultice on her chest. "I'll be better soon, Ion. You're a good boy," she said, giving him the empty cup. "I only want one thing, and that is to see dear Lucian and Tantza, just once before I die. I have asked God for this many times, Ion, but with no result. It is such a long time since they were here, and my old heart aches for them, as it has for many years."

Ion looked out of the window at the rough road outside. Then he knew what he must do. He must find his parents. They had been taken away when he was two years old, by the police, and he had never seen them again. Often he had imagined them in prison, or in one of the asylums, where people who disagreed with the government were sent and there made insane— or those were the stories people told to one another in whispers, always afraid that there

3

might be an informer in their midst. For now—adays no one knew whom they could trust. Even Vasile, who had lived in the village his whole life, was suspected of being an informer because he had turned up in a new suit. As for Stefan, everyone knew that he was a secret policeman. Once he had been as poor as the rest of them, had labored in the fields with them from dawn to sunset. Then he had started working elsewhere, and almost overnight he had acquired a car, which was something beyond most people's wildest dreams. Most recently he had been seen eating oranges. And his hands were clean and there was always money in his pockets. All the same Ion could not help admiring Stefan. Once he had given Ion a lift in his car and another time a banana. He had talked about things no one else in the village mentioned—about space, and guns with special bullets that shot down airplanes in the dark.

So now, Ion thought, I'll see Stefan. He'll help me. I'll ask him to contact Uncle Fanel in

England. Perhaps then my uncle will come in his smart camper and help us. For the next few hours he clung to that hope. He imagined Uncle Fanel and his family arriving with food; there would be laughter again in the old house then, and wine, but most of all hope.

When Ion went to the village pump for water, everyone asked the same thing: "How is the old lady?" and Ion answered, "Just the same." But they hardly heard him, for their minds were on the huge bulldozers parked just outside the village. "They've come to demolish our village like they have a thousand other villages," they said. "Perhaps it will be better for your grandmother to die, Ion. She's too old to start again in an apartment." Disheartened, Ion left them and went in search of Stefan, who was washing his car.

"Grandmother is dying and I need help," he said desperately.

"We all die in time," Stefan replied without looking up.

"I want your help, please," Ion insisted. "Can

you ring my uncle in England? I know he'll help. You have a telephone, you can get through. Please, Stefan, it's my only hope."

Stefan stopped washing his car and looked at Ion. "I can't do it. I can't afford to talk to people in the West. Do you think I want to be sent to prison like your parents, Ion?" he shouted, and now he too looked around to see if anyone might be listening. "I'm sorry I can't help you, Ion," he continued, still in a loud voice, as a peasant woman with a cow passed by.

"I'll give you some money," Ion said. "And Grandma has jewelry."

"I need dollars, no other currency is any use to me. Now go away and leave me alone. Do you hear? Go!" Stefan shouted.

Walking away, Ion thought, he's scared too. We're all scared. And then he knew what he had to do—he had to find his parents himself and bring them home.

Peasants were still standing around the pump. "No luck, then?" Maria called. "I'm not surprised. Stefan wouldn't help anyone, not even his own mother." So she had guessed what he was doing, he thought. The other peasants were still talking about the expected destruction of the village, for no one wanted to live in the enormous blocks of apartment buildings, which were appearing almost overnight to replace their small beloved houses.

"I'll take my pig with me, she can live on the landing," an old man said.

"You should have gone with your uncle when he came here," said Maria. "You would have been all right then, Ion."

As if I don't know that now, thought Ion bitterly. He still couldn't bear to recall that time when he had set off for England, and then returned to his grandmother when a revolution began. It had seemed the right thing to do at the time, but the leaders of the revolution had vanished, nobody knew where, and things had been growing worse ever since, until now in some parts of the country children were dying of hunger.

Another minute and Ion was standing by his

grandmother's bed saying, "I'm going to find my parents, okay?"

She nodded while he added, "I'll come back with medicine and a doctor. You do understand what I'm saying, don't you? I'm going to leave you."

"Yes, and I too want to see them; it is my dying wish," said the old lady. "Bring them back to me, but first go and see Mr. Ditescu. He'll advise you. Go now. I will be all right, I'll manage."

Mr. Ditescu was the schoolmaster, an old man now, and a relation—a man you could trust, who dreamed of a king returning to rule the country. He'd lived alone since his wife had died many years ago. He once had a car, which had rusted away waiting for spare parts.

Ion looked at his grandmother and saw again how ill she was. As he ran toward Mr. Ditescu's house he thought, if I don't hurry, the village will be gone forever when I return and Grandma will be dead.

2

Ion Says Good-bye

Mr. DITESCU WAS surprised to see Ion. He thought his grandmother must have died and started to talk about the cost of a coffin. Ion was not used to talking to him; he was used to him standing in the classroom giving orders, saying: "Get out your books." "Take down what I tell you." That sort of thing.

Now Ion looked at Mr. Ditescu with nervous eyes and said, "Mr. Ditescu, I have not come here about my grandmother. I have come because I need your help to find my parents."

Mr. Ditescu had large eyebrows and a large mustache. Once they had been black, but the years had turned them gray. There were wrinkles around his tired brown eyes. He looked big and cross, like a bear woken from a deep sleep, Ion thought.

"I wouldn't do that, Ion, I really wouldn't attempt it," he said. "It could land you in a lot of trouble, my boy."

"I'm in trouble already. My grandmother is dying and I have no one to help me; and if she dies I'll be sent to an orphanage, and you know what will happen to me then: either I'll be starved to death or I'll have to become a secret policeman," replied Ion, staring at Mr. Ditescu. "And I don't want to be a policeman."

Mr. Ditescu went to his small, grimy window and looked out. He knew what Ion said was true. "A policeman's life isn't so bad, if you keep to the rules," he said.

"But I don't want to keep to the rules," cried Ion. "I hate the rules."

Mr. Ditescu saw now that Ion was determined to leave the village and find his parents. He admired him for his courage. He was also afraid for him. He knew what happened to people who asked questions. "It won't be easy. They may be dead. Have you thought of that?" he asked.

"Yes, a thousand times, but I still don't believe it," cried Ion. "Anyway, we had a note from them ages ago, saying they were alive. Besides, I must know one way or the other. Can't you see?"

"There is going to be a revolution. And who will look after your grandmother while you are away?" asked Mr. Ditescu over his shoulder, pacing his small cluttered room.

"Maria," Ion said. "And Vasile, and Nina."

"Well, if you must leave, I suggest you go to Party Headquarters in the town and ask there for your parents," advised Mr. Ditescu.

Ion knew the building; he had passed it several times, always uneasily, looking over his shoulder to make sure that he was not being followed.

"And then?" he asked now, staring at Mr. Ditescu in a way he had never looked at him before, seeing him differently, as someone growing old and fearful, sad too; someone who lived alone with his books and his memories.

"Ask. Explain that your grandmother is dying. But be careful, don't lose your temper. Be polite, Ion, or you too will disappear," said Mr. Ditescu, sounding concerned and pulling at his mustache with fingers stained with nicotine. Mr. Ditescu wished that he could offer Ion something to eat, but he had nothing besides a loaf of bread in his house. So he only said, "Be very, very careful. Remember that such officials have great power, Ion. A wrong word from you and you're finished. They're more dangerous than the fiercest wild animal, so watch your tongue, my boy. Don't speak out of turn, and if the revolution starts return straight home."

Ion thanked him and went back along the muddy road to his home. He told his grandmother that he would be leaving at daybreak to walk to the town and would make inquiries there.

"It's such a big building, someone must know where they are," he said.

He didn't feel frightened because he was glad

to be doing something at last. Besides, he was tired of looking after his sick grandmother. And he didn't want to be there when she died. He knew it was wrong, but he couldn't change his feelings. He wanted to feel free, if only for a short time. He wanted to be himself.

After he had milked the cow again and locked up the geese, Ion went to see Maria. "I am leaving you in charge of my grandmother," he said on entering her small house, where the walls were hung with colorful rugs and the tables covered with embroidered cloths.

"You have some nerve, Ion. Maybe I don't want to look after your grandmother," replied Maria, who had curly hair and a large mouth. She had once been rosy-cheeked and laughing, but was now tired and often sullen.

"Please, Maria. I have to find my parents. You can have all the milk from the cow, and eat as many of our chickens as you like. I won't be long," Ion said. "And you will be rewarded in heaven, Maria. I know you will."

"But you won't find them. You're wasting

your time. You will be shot yourself, or put in prison, Ion. And what will happen to your grandmother then?" asked Maria. "People say there's going to be another revolution."

"Please, Maria. I'm only going to Party Headquarters. I may even be back the same day," Ion pleaded.

"I've seen the bulldozers, they are on their way. We're going to be moved," said Maria. "They are going to dig big holes and knock our little houses into them. I shall lose everything, and so will you."

"Please."

"We're going to lose our land. It will all be given to the cooperative farm." Maria was crying now. Ion had never seen her cry before. He was rooted to where he stood. "I'll speak to them at Party Headquarters," he said after a moment. "I will ask them why. I'll make them change their minds, Maria, I promise."

"Change their minds? They can't. It's the President's orders. But thank you for saying it, Ion. Of course, I'll look after your grandmother, but come back soon. Promise me that, Ion. And keep out of trouble." She kissed him on the cheek. She smelled of garlic, cow, and homemade soap. She was part of his childhood, of growing up, for she had always been there, like the small river and the rickety bridge and the vineyard on the hill. She was as much part of him as the village. She had no husband. No children. People said that her husband had left her for a Gypsy woman. Ever since that day she had nursed the sick in the village and seen to the dead.

Now Ion said, "Thank you, Maria," and left her house. The geese were cackling in their shed as he passed by, softly, like people talking. The moon was high in the sky and a million stars looked down on him.

His grandmother was coughing when he reached home again. "Bring me some brandy, son," she said. He wasn't her son, but recently she had started to call him that. It made him realize that her mind was wandering, going back into the past, and it worried him.

Her hands were cold as ice and the fire in the

stove was almost out. He was worried now at leaving her, but he knew he had to go. It was his only hope. Her old withered hands curled round the glass he gave her. Then she told him to open the top drawer of the chest of drawers and take out the photographs. "Choose the best, my son," she said.

There were many there, with his father in each one of them. After a time he chose the one of his father and mother standing together outside the house in which he now stood. They had built it with their own hands, making the bricks themselves out of mud and straw, then baking them under a hot summer sun. Next his grandmother handed him an envelope from under her pillow. "There's money inside it, Ion. Use it carefully," she said. "And don't be too long, son."

He drank a mugful of milk fresh from the cow and ate a hunk of bread. "Once they're found I'll come straight back," he said. "They'll stop the bulldozers, I know they will. They'll save us."

"And if they're not found?"

"I'll come back just the same."

Neither of them put into words what they were thinking, which was, to return may be impossible and we may never see each other again.

Ion went to bed. It was very cold outside. The village dogs were barking; otherwise all was silent. He felt he was saying good-bye to everything forever. And because things always appear worse in the small hours of the night, he saw himself imprisoned and tortured with half his fingers gone. He couldn't sleep and was relieved when at last dawn broke with a crowing of cocks and a mooing of cows.

When the time came for Ion to leave, some of the peasants were waiting to wave him goodbye. One gave him a small handkerchief as a keepsake; another, sandwiches wrapped in a cloth. They wished him luck. Saying good-bye to his grandmother had not been easy; now she stood by the door watching. Dressed in black with a shawl around her shoulders and her hair twisted into a knot at the back of her head, she called, "God bless you, Ion. Bring back my son."

It was very quiet in the village; the cocks had stopped crowing. Men were leaving, silent and surly, to go to work. Maria hugged him. "Don't worry. I'll see to everything," she said. Even Mr. Ditescu was standing at his window and raised a hand in farewell.

Ion had put the money and photograph in an inside pocket of his coat. He had a cap on his head and shoes, but his feet were wrapped in rags because he had no socks. His trousers were patched clumsily by his grandmother, whose eyesight was failing. Only his shirt was respectable. And as for gloves, he had none. He tried to hurry, but his heart was heavy with leaving and his mind was anxious. Soon his shoes, which were old and outgrown, started to rub his heels, while his mind said to him, "You'll never find them, however hard you try. Too much time has passed. You won't recognize them either. You will be like a stranger. You've left it too long. You are too late, Ion."

3

"Kill Me Too"

THERE WERE SOLDIERS grouped around two trucks on the road to Augusta. They were fitting snow chains to the wheels and talking about revolution. Ion did not believe in revolutions. He had been mixed up in one once before and it had come to nothing. Then there was to have been an amnesty and the whole village had hoped that his parents would be set free. But the only result had been a dirty scrap of paper in an envelope that had arrived one morning by post, which read: WE ARE STILL ALIVE. Nothing more, not even an address, and though his grandmother had made some inquiries, in great fear and secrecy, not another word had been heard from them. Twice after that Ion had dreamed that they were blind-

19

folded with their arms tied behind their backs, waiting to be shot. In the second dream he had been actually awakened by the sound of the gunfire in his head.

Now one of the soldiers on the road to Augusta said, "I'll support the President," while another one announced loudly, "I will obey orders." Ion could see guns and a machine gun in the trucks. Nearby, an old woman stood gesticulating. She looked so familiar she might have come from Ion's own village, but he had never seen her before. She took hold of a soldier's arm, crying, "You have destroyed my house; you killed my husband when he tried to stop you. Where am I to keep my animals, you fiends? What about my two cows, my old pony, my fowl? How am I to live?"

And a soldier replied, "We were obeying orders. You'll be better off in your new apartment." Ion thought that she must have no reason for living to speak so recklessly.

"I don't understand, comrades," she continued in a tormented voice. "I have always believed in the Party until now."

There was a lot Ion did not understand either, he thought as he left them still talking, but he tried not to think about these things. He kept telling himself that he had a job to do, and must not get involved in other things, but as he walked along the snowy road, he couldn't help thinking about the old woman's animals without shelter.

Presently he heard a wailing siren, and a police car rushed by, skidding dangerously on the icy road, while in the distance factory chimneys belched smoke into the clear winter sky. A minute later he smelled fumes polluting the atmosphere, and soon after that he heard gunfire. With a sinking heart, he thought: there *is* a revolution, and I'm walking straight into it. For an awful moment fear gripped him. Then he knew he had to go on, that nothing would make him go back and confess, "I couldn't find them." If he did, he knew everyone would try to conceal their feelings, his grandmother most of all, but they would be there just the same—

the disappointment, the grief, the years of unshed tears continuing just the same. And as for Mr. Ditescu telling him to return at once if there was a revolution, he forgot all about that.

The town was looming nearer all the time. Soon the fumes from the chimneys entered his lungs and seared his throat. He could hear the sound of more gunfire. He knew the way to Party Headquarters, everyone did. It was the largest and most palatial building in the whole of Augusta. To be called there always meant trouble; nobody ever returned unscathed. Once it had been a prince's palace. Today everything was different—there were no guards outside the entrance; but the very change made Ion feel even sicker inside. There was no one about, and when he stepped inside all he could smell was burning paper.

As he walked up the wide, empty staircase, he kept rehearsing what he intended saying. It was this: "Honorable Sir, I am inquiring about my parents. Their names are Lucian and

Tantza Radu." He had imagined many answers. He had even imagined himself marched down a long corridor to be interrogated. He had imagined himself standing with a bright light shining on him day and night, naked, not knowing what to say, how to confess to something he knew nothing about. Recently the very thought had made him wake in the night in a cold sweat. Now it was happening. And nothing was as he had imagined! He thought, if only I wasn't alone. Doors were open. Room after room was empty, with drawers ransacked and paper burning in ancient elaborate fireplaces. There were open bottles of wine half drunk and half-smoked cigarettes smoldering in ashtrays. Room after room was the same, while under Ion's feet the wall-to-wall carpeting was as thick as summer grass.

At last he stopped outside a closed door with the name Colonel Cazacu written on it. He knocked timidly and went inside. Colonel Cazacu was sitting by his desk, a bottle of plum brandy beside him. His feet rested on a chair; his gray hair looked rumpled. He had undone the belt on his jacket and had a revolver in his hand.

Ion took off his cap and bowed, and then said, "Honorable Sir, I am inquiring about my parents, Lucian and Tantza Radu."

Colonel Cazacu looked him up and down with bleary eyes. "You're looking for your parents, is that what you are saying?" he asked, looking hard at Ion.

Ion nodded while a small flicker of hope rose inside him.

Then the colonel laughed and smashed his wine glass against the wall and his laughter grew louder and louder until the whole room shook with it, and then as quickly he subsided into drunken tears. "Go outside and look. They're killing us. What do your parents matter now we are all doomed to the lunatics out there? The old order has gone. We're finished," he sobbed.

Ion went to the window and looked down,

and now he could see a great crowd gathering, and they were all shouting one word: "Freedom."

The very word seemed to light a candle in his heart before he turned to look at the drunken colonel and thought, I'm glad you're finished. I hope you all die. "So you can't help me, old man?" he asked with insolence in his voice.

"No," shouted the colonel, banging the table. "Go away, you miserable peasant, go back to where you belong. Do you hear me—go."

Outside, the corridor was suddenly full of young men. There was blood on the stairs and someone had slashed the portraits on the walls with a knife. Ion ran down the stairs and out into the street, where there were people everywhere shouting and wielding all sorts of weapons. Shop windows were smashed and burning cars blocked the road. And now Ion did not know which way to go or what to do. He knew only one thing—he wasn't returning home until he had found his parents, and if he died trying to find them, it wouldn't matter because nothing mattered now as much as finding them. And so, as he pushed through the crowd, he kept imagining their faces: his father's heavily mustached, his mother's beautiful, with eyes like almonds. Small for his age, Ion could see little but legs of all shapes and sizes, and soon he was being carried along by the crowd, almost suffocating in the uproar, while the cry went on and on: "Freedom, freedom, freedom."

Next, tanks thundered through the town. Flags were burned. A woman screamed, bewailing the death of her son. And now Ion could only think, where am I going next? What am I to do? He had thought it would be easy to find his parents. He had said he might even return that very day. What a fool he had been!

Suddenly the tanks started to fire and the crowd scattered in all directions. Ion was knocked down and got up again and ran he knew not where, while a man shouted,

"They're killing us. God help us. They're our brothers." He was a very tall man, with a very large coat that flapped around him like black wings. He was like a vampire in a nightmare, Ion thought as the man waved his arms and shouted, "Don't shoot us, comrades." And then he fell and lay quite still, struck by a hail of bullets. Ion's heart was banging like a sledge-hammer now and he thought, I should have turned back on the road to Augusta. I should have listened to Mr. Ditescu.

But now a woman was standing in front of a tank. She was thirty-two years old, but looked much younger. She waved a flag fearlessly and cried, "Come on, kill me." It was the bravest act Ion had ever witnessed—the very sight gave him courage. He thought, death doesn't matter, it's how you die that counts. Most people had fled, so that now the street was almost empty. Ion crossed it, and standing beside the woman, cried, "Kill me. Come on, kill me too!"

Inside the tank the soldiers were young, with

bland, unlined faces. They didn't know what to do.

"They won't kill us, now they don't feel threatened," the woman said, smiling at Ion. "I'm Cristina. Who are you?"

"Ion Radu."

"From the country?"

"Yes, I'm looking for my parents. It's rather urgent. You see, my grandmother is dying. I wonder if you know them. I have a photograph," Ion said, unbuttoning his coat and putting his hand inside the pocket there.

"Not now," she replied. She had a gun slung across her shoulder, and boots from another land, smart and pointed. A pink outfit. Blond hair. Ion wanted to say, "You're very beautiful." He wanted to kiss her small hand. He wished he was wearing better clothes; he wished he had a smart cap on his head and smart shoes on his feet. Another moment and Cristina was exchanging cigarettes with the tank crew. She looked at home with them. Ion thought she would look at home anywhere.

Then, glancing in his direction, she said, "Buzz off. Go home. I'm busy—all right?"

Ion did up his coat, but he didn't go. Instead, he said, "I have to find my parents. I am lost and know no one. They're in prison and I want to take them home."

She continued talking to the soldiers, ignoring him. Everything was quiet now. The guns had stopped firing. A weeping woman with a scarf covering her hair was tenderly placing flowers and a lighted candle near a wall.

Ion waited. He had waited so long for his parents, a few more hours hardly counted. Besides, he was used to waiting—for cows to finish eating, for his turn at the village pump, for the mush to be cooked on the stove at home. He would have liked to sit down. But this was not the country and there was no bank to sit on, just hard, cracked, bloodstained tarmac beneath his feet. So he waited for Cristina to finish talking, and as he waited evening came to the unhappy town.

At last Cristina stopped and turned to him.

"Goodness, are you still here? Why don't you go home?" she asked, giving him a small, impatient push.

"I have no home. My parents are in prison. I have to find them," Ion replied. (Saying that he had no home seemed only a small lie, so surely it wasn't a sin, he thought.)

"Have you no relations here?" Cristina asked crossly.

"No, madam," he said. "I am quite alone. I have nothing but a few sandwiches in my pocket, a photograph of my parents, and a little money."

"You must have come from somewhere," Cristina retorted angrily, walking on along the street.

"But I can't go back. Can't you see? I can't go back without my parents," cried Ion, seizing hold of her pink jacket. "I am an orphan without my parents. I have no hope. I shall be made into a secret policeman."

"A good one, I hope. Because we are killing the others, Ion," she replied, laughing.

"Point me to a prison, tell me where to go,

please, Cristina," Ion pleaded. "My parents have been in prison for years and years. Look, I have a photograph. It was taken a long time ago, but they may not have changed too much." His voice trailed away. She was not listening. He held on to her jacket, his hard, grubby hand tightly clenched. His stomach rumbled with hunger. A crowd was singing the national anthem—the old forbidden one. Ion had heard it once before at the other revolution. And now he could see that everything was changing. The prisons might be opening for all he knew. He had to hurry. A few more days and anything could happen. The President might even order that all prisoners be shot. He was capable of anything; everyone knew that. He had reigned for so long that many people almost admired him; he was there, high above them like the devil. For years he had been like the weather, unalterable. He had done as he liked. Ion was filled with panic now. Suddenly Cristina was his only hope. Without her he knew no one. He was lost in a sea of people, without one familiar face among them. He was frightened, so frightened that his blood really did run cold inside him.

"You must help me, please, Cristina," he pleaded, shivering. Then, for an awful moment, he wished that he had never set out on this venture, that he was still at home nursing his sick grandmother, with the village all around him, cocooning him against the horrors of life. He wanted Maria to pick him up in her sturdy arms and say, "It's all right, Ion. I'm here," as she had so often when he was younger.

"You can't leave me, Cristina, not now, please," he said next.

She relented at last with a sigh. "Very well," she said, "you can come with me. But keep your head down. Do you understand?"

He did not understand, but nodded just the same, overcome with a sudden flood of gratitude. "You won't be sorry. I promise you," he said. And now everything seemed better. Hope rushed back, raising his spirits. Warmth seeped through his veins. "I'll keep my head down, I promise," he said.

Cristina hurried. Ion had to run to keep up with her. "Where are we going?" he asked after a time.

"To meet my students," she replied.

He knew she didn't like him asking questions because every time he did, she sighed. But he wanted to know more; he wanted to know why a blond woman like herself was carrying a gun. In his village the women were quite different. They were dark-haired and strong. They were capable of killing animals and shouting at the men when they were drunk. But not one had a gun; guns were for the men in their village.

"I am a university lecturer," Cristina explained. "There. Are you surprised?"

And of course, Ion did not know how to answer, could only nod his head and mutter, "I knew you were important."

"We've been plotting this revolution for

years. Many have been arrested. Now it has happened, and sooner or later the President will be caught and dealt with in a suitable manner," she said next.

"And then we'll be free," cried Ion hopefully.

"I hope so," she answered. "But it won't be easy, and it isn't over yet. We may still lose."

"And then you'll be shot?"

"Maybe . . ."

Ion thought that she was the most courageous person he had ever met and the most beautiful. He would have liked her as a relation, a close one. He would have liked her to come and live in his village and sort out the problems there. "Could you be President? You would be a good one," he said, hoping to please her.

"Don't flatter me," she said, walking faster.

"Where are we going?" Ion asked next. "I have to find my parents and I do not think we are going in the right direction." He was wishing that he had a present to give her, a perfectly worked tablecloth perhaps, or a basket made by his own hands.

"Your parents must wait. I am joining my students, and we're going to march on the main square. You can do as you please, Ion, stay or go."

And after a short pause Ion replied, "I'll stay with you. But please, can I have a gun?"

4

The Revolution

THEY CAME TO a side street where a crowd had gathered. A young man with a beard stepped forward to embrace Cristina.

"But who have you brought with you? Do I see a peasant boy?" he asked, stepping back to stare at Ion.

"I can't shake him off, and he may be useful. Who knows?" replied Cristina with a shrug.

"You mean they may be peasants themselves and not want to kill one of themselves," said the young man with a laugh.

"He's looking for his parents," explained Cristina.

"Aren't we all in one way or another?" replied the young man.

"Honorable Sir, I would like a gun. I would like to kill the men who have imprisoned my parents for so many years," said Ion boldly. "I have fired a gun before and I am not afraid."

"You speak like a bantam cock, but we have no guns to spare," the young man said as they moved out of the side street into the square, where they unfurled mutilated flags and started to march four abreast with Ion wedged in the third row, still longing for a gun. Surrounded as he was by thirty or forty people, Ion felt quite brave and though he was not getting any nearer to his parents, he was satisfied to be where he was. He thought that Mr. Ditescu would be impressed if he could see him now, and maybe his grandfather was looking down from heaven admiringly. He thought, my parents will have to wait a little longer. And then he thought, but if I die I'll never see them again.

Some of the students smelled of drink. Some had red faces; others appeared pale and tense. Not that Ion could see much, being so much smaller than they were. The red-faced ones laughed, the others were almost silent, and so they marched into the square, which had a small fountain in the middle and a statue of the President. They faced the tanks, prepared to die if they must. The tank commander, a burly man in battle fatigues, cried, "Halt and lay down your weapons."

They stopped and looked at him without faltering and no one laid down a weapon. Ion could hear the beating of hearts all around him, his own loudest of all. He was filled with tremendous excitement, and his blood really did run faster. And so they waited, looking down the barrels of the guns pointing at them, knowing that an order to fire would kill them all. Ion imagined them falling like ninepins; his own lonely grave, his grandmother dying as she waited for his return, ignorant of his untimely fate. But he did not break ranks, just waited while Cristina stepped forward and spoke to the tank commander.

She said that they were all brothers and comrades. She said that they all knew it was time for change, for democracy to take root and flower, and then she looked at Ion and asked, "Would you really gun down this boy who is searching for his parents long imprisoned by the President? Like many of us here, he comes from a humble village. His feet are wrapped in rags. He cannot afford socks. And he has no parents, the President has seen to that," she continued.

Ion felt both proud and humbled by her remarks.

Some of the soldiers laughed; others looked embarrassed. Then one cried, "We won't fire. We're with you. Down with the President!"

And another shouted, "I'm from a village too and my people are starving."

Before long, bystanders started to shout and cheer, then to stone the statue of the President. The soldiers got down from their tanks. The commander embraced Cristina. And then quite suddenly the firing began, not from the tanks, but from men in plain clothes, who had been watching—secret policemen. The bearded young man fell at once and so did others. The remaining students fired back, not very accurately, it is true, but enough to make the policemen flee across the square.

"After them," yelled Cristina.

"Murderers," shouted someone else.

Ion ran after Cristina, who was still firing her gun, stopping only to reload, and he kept thinking, if only I had a gun too!

The policemen were scattering, and one lay wounded in the square. The statue of the President had been toppled and the tanks were leaving. Cristina was chasing one particular policeman now, and presently he ran into a house, firing as he ran.

"Go away, Ion. You'll get hurt," Cristina shouted over her shoulder.

"Never," replied Ion.

"Go on, scram."

But Ion had nowhere to go and ran on, through the house, through iron doors and down into a tunnel, and now it was like a bad dream, but worse because it was real, and all the time he was losing ground, for Cristina ran too fast for him. He was afraid he would be left behind, forgotten, entombed for ever and ever. He felt sick with fear as the distance widened between him and Cristina, until he lost sight of her altogether. He slowed to a walk then and saw that the tunnel held many things—guns and ammunition, filing cabinets, typewriters, reams of paper. Other tunnels led out of it. He thought, if there's no food or drink down here I'll starve to death if I don't get out, and what a way to die, trapped like an animal underneath the city.

Next, Ion thought, if only my legs were longer, I could have kept up. Then he muttered, "Holy Mother of God, help me. I am too young to die. I want to see my parents. I want to go back to my village. I will never do anything wicked if only you will save me. Please God, if you exist, do something." Then he thought, I'm finished. They will slam a gate shut and forget all about me, or I will go round and round these tunnels and never find a way out. He started to shout, "Cristina, come back." Suddenly his prayers seemed answered because Cristina returned, saying, "I've lost the secret policeman. We're going to the capital. They need us there."

"But what about my parents?" Ion asked. "I have to find them." And his voice was plaintive because he was so tired and so hungry.

"We'll find them. They're not here. They're miles away. We'll make inquiries in the capital. Or would you rather go back to your village? You don't have to come with us, you know," she said, looking at him with hazel eyes, the most beautiful eyes he had ever seen.

"I can't go back," Ion replied. "Not until I've found my parents. It's just not possible."

"We will go on then, but hurry," Cristina said.

Then he remembered the food the peasants had given him, and he ate it as he walked. They left the tunnel and came out into the light, blinking like rabbits from their burrows, or moles from their runs beneath the earth.

It was evening now. The streets were dark, for the lamps there rarely worked due to lack of electricity. The tanks had been recalled to barracks, Cristina said, because no one could trust the soldiers to kill their brothers anymore. The tall, bearded young man was no longer lying in a puddle of blood in the square. All around, the houses were shuttered and barred.

The students were waiting in a truck. They helped Ion inside while Cristina joined the driver in the cab. No one sang now, just passed round bread and wine and small pieces of cheese. The inside of the truck smelled of anxiety and of tired unwashed bodies. All the men had stubble on their chins and the only woman besides Cristina had a bandaged head and a bloodstained face. Ion could not help thinking, this is real, it's really happening, and I am here in the forefront. One day I shall be able to tell my children about it, if I live long enough to have children.

Ion must have slept, for the next thing he saw was a morning sky, gray and pink, and the snow-topped roofs of the capital.

The truck stopped and they all went into an apartment and washed. They were a sorry lot, some with bloodstained faces and all with dirt on them and tangled hair. Most of them had slept in the truck and were still bleary with sleep. They were all hungry. The hunger was now a dull ache in Ion's side that would not go away. It made his legs weak and his head fuzzy. No one spoke, not even Cristina, who was still beautiful in spite of the dirt. Then bread was found and torn in pieces and eaten, and coffee was brewed that tasted of something that was not coffee. Ion marveled at the hot water that flowed from the taps in the apartment. He was impressed by the flush toilet and the stove in the kitchen. With the food and coffee inside him, he felt his courage returning. Soon there was a sound like swarming bees outside and everyone stood up, reaching for weapons with stiff arms.

"Why don't you stay here and sleep, Ion?" asked Cristina. But Ion wouldn't stay, for now he felt he belonged with these people as he belonged to the village.

They tried to persuade him, but he stood stubbornly shouting, "No, no, no," until Cristina said wearily, "Oh, let him come. He may be useful. One never knows."

There was an immense crowd outside now and banners that read DOWN WITH COMMUNISM and LIBERTY being carried and waved and hanging from walls. In the distance high up on a balcony, someone was trying to speak. "He's the President," Cristina explained.

"But he's so ordinary. He doesn't look like a president," Ion replied in wonder, and thought, Vasile or Uncle Fanel could push him over. Why have we been frightened of him for so long? There was so much noise now that even with a microphone in place, no one could hear the fur-hatted President, who soon gave up. Then someone else took his place and called for calm, and was booed and catcalled while the crowd grew and grew. Then fighting began. Soon there were skirmishes at every corner, and Ion could not understand who was fighting whom, and all the time voices were calling

"Liberty," even as people fell. The fearless crowd kept growing larger and there were foreigners too, spilling out of big hotels, cameras filming. Ion was overcome by it all. He had never been in such a situation before and was still overwhelmed by the thought that the President looked so ordinary and yet had filled the whole nation with fear for as long as he could remember. He wanted to ask someone, "What's happening? Who is killing whom?" But everyone was too busy to answer. And all the while he had the feeling that he should be somewhere else.

Then a great cry went up: "The army is with us. The President has fled." And there were cheers and shouts. Then bottles of wine were opened and drunk and everyone started singing and locking arms, men in uniform as well as everyone else.

Someone lifted Ion onto a man's shoulders as the cheering went on and on, and then quite suddenly the gunfire began again, and everyone started to flee. Ion fell to the ground and was trampled on and the square ran with blood while snow fell like torn paper from the sky. Soon the square echoed with the cries of the fallen. Trampled banners and torn flags lay everywhere.

A soldier picked up Ion. He'll take me to prison now; but if my parents are there I won't mind, Ion thought. And his head was spinning and his right arm was aching. "Go home. Go home at once," the soldier said. "Go home and put up the shutters and lie on the ground. Do you hear me? Go home."

Ion would have liked to say, "I'm lost and my home is miles and miles away and probably demolished by now. So, as you see, I am all alone." But he was too afraid to speak. So, muttering "Thank you," he walked away and looked for the apartment where he had washed, and eaten bread and drunk coffee, but he could not find it.

The square was almost empty now. A mixture of blood and wine trickled between paving stones and all the houses were barred and shuttered as they had been in Augusta. There were three dead men lying at a street corner and a dead woman, who had lost a shoe. Ion averted his eyes when he saw them. He did not know where to go or what to do. His arm ached, his teeth ached; there was blood in his mouth and his bottom lip was swelling. And he had not found the smallest sign of his parents anywhere.

5

The Search Begins

ION WALKED ROUND and round the square, not knowing where to go next, until the man who had put him on his shoulders in the square reappeared and said, "Come with me. I'm Cristina's friend. I saw you with her." He had fair hair like Cristina and spoke her way, which was not the way the peasants spoke in Ion's village. "She's resting and we're regrouping. The army is with us now. It will soon be over," he explained. Ion followed the man. "They are pursuing the President. The army will soon have him," he continued. Ion remembered the President, who was so ordinary, and thought, I hope they shoot him, and knew he should not think like that, but couldn't help it.

They went in an elevator, up and up to where Cristina was, clean and smelling of flowers, and Ion saw himself in the big mirror in the hall there and saw how terrible he looked with dirty face and swollen lip, and blood and dirt on his shoes. Cristina looked at him and laughed. "You must have a bath. You are dirtying my carpets," she said. And to Ion's now-infatuated ears her laugh was like the tinkling of a brook on a summer's day.

"I don't want to fight anymore. I want to find my parents. I've made up my mind. I can't go back without them," replied Ion stubbornly.

She laughed again and ran water into a bath that was as white as the snow outside. Ion had never seen such a bath before, nor such taps. While he was in it Cristina washed his head and back, which embarrassed him, and threw away the rags that had bound his feet. She found him shoes and clean socks and a warm plaid scarf. A year or two ago he would have been delighted with such presents. Now he was ashamed and humiliated by them. Next, she took almost-new trousers and a jacket from a drawer and said, "Try these for size."

They fitted. Everything fitted. "Once I had a son, but he died," she said later, frying him an egg. "He went to the hospital with an infection and they gave him bad blood. Perhaps they wanted to kill him, who knows? Fortunately I have relations in the West, so I haven't been arrested."

"Couldn't they have helped?" Ion asked after a moment.

"There wasn't time. But I'm glad I've found a home for his clothes. For a long time I have been searching for someone worthy of them," she said.

Ion took her hand and kissed it, as was customary in his village when a present was given, or a farewell said. "I would be honored if you would come to our village. We would give you the best of everything," he told her gravely.

Ion wanted to leave after he had eaten. "I must find my mother and father. If I leave it too long my grandmother will be dead," he said.

"But it is impossible. Look, it is night," Cristina cried, opening the shutters. "I will draw you a map in the morning. The telephone doesn't work. Journalists are telephoning from hotels and have jammed the lines. I would like to have made inquiries for you."

Ion was not used to speaking by telephone. Stefan had one and there was one on the main road, but he had never used either. Cristina found him pajamas and he went to bed in a modern bed that was quite different from the one he used at home. He slept the deep sleep of complete exhaustion. There were no cocks to wake him in the morning, crowing their hearts out, so he slept on untroubled until Cristina shook him awake, saying, "It's another day, Ion. And today we must find your parents."

"They've arrested the President," Cristina said as later he ate a breakfast of bread spread with thick, sweet jam, and drank the coffee that tasted of something else.

"Will they shoot him?"

"I expect so. Now we must hunt down the

secret policemen who were killing us yesterday. They are trained killers; they'll disappear
underground and live in the sewers like rats, so
they must be liquidated," she said.

Ion imagined Stefan being caught. Would
they shoot him too? It wasn't a nice thought. He
stood up and took his breakfast things to the
sink. Cristina handed him a map and a package
with food in it for the journey. He kissed her
hand. She kissed his cheek.

"Will I ever see you again?" he asked.

"Only time will tell. Good luck," she said.

He felt very lonely going down in the elevator with the map in his pocket and the money
and the photograph transferred from his old
clothes to an inside pocket in his new jacket.
His new shoes didn't fit as well as the old. They
were pointed and his feet were broad from
walking barefoot.

Soon he looked at the map. The prison she
had drawn for him appeared to be only a few
miles from the city, so he could walk there. On
the edge of the map Cristina had written her

address and telephone number. Beneath them she had written: CONTACT ME IF YOU ARE IN TROUBLE.

He wished he could have stayed longer. He reached the main square and took the road that led out of the town toward distant hills. And so at last the real search began. The road was empty, as though everyone was still recovering from yesterday. He passed looted shops, burned-out cars, even a charred tank, which sent a shiver down his spine. I've wasted two whole days because of the revolution, he thought, and caught his reflection in an unbroken window and saw that he looked quite different in his new clothes, not a peasant anymore. He didn't know whether to be pleased or sorry. But, maybe because of the clothes, he felt more cheerful than he had in days and saw himself returning home in triumph. What a lot I will have to tell Grandmother, Mr. Ditescu, Vasile, and Maria, he thought. But will they believe me? And his walk became a jog and the mountains grew nearer as he left the capital behind.

Several miles passed before he saw the prison in the distance, unmistakable with high wire fences and watchtowers coated with snow. A weak winter sun shone down on him as three cars went by full of army officers. A river lay white and cold beneath the mountains before the road curved and climbed uphill. Nothing could dishearten Ion now because suddenly he was filled with unexpected hope. He found himself whistling as he approached the prison, though what tune he whistled he never could recall afterward. Then when he saw the gates he ran, skidding on the icy road in his new pointed shoes. The soldiers outside wore gray uniforms and fur hats. He was surprised to see them still there. He had been certain that they had all been recalled to the barracks. In his head he prepared what he would say. Then he bowed a little and said, "Excuse me, I am sorry to trouble you, but I have come about my parents. I wish to see them."

They waved him through the gates, telling him to go to Reception. "Ring the bell there," they said.

But Ion did not ring the bell. Instead he walked around outside the wire, peering at the prisoners locked out in the snow wearing thin, striped, pajama-like clothes. They looked a weary, motley lot. Twice Ion thought he saw his mother, but when he looked again he wasn't certain, for no one looked like the photograph he carried. Their hair was roughly shorn and their eyes had a hopeless look in them, quite unlike the almond-shaped eyes that looked so confident in the photograph. They're broken, all broken people, Ion thought sadly, going to the main door, pulling the bell, listening to it tinkling along endless, cold, empty corridors. And now his heart sank fast into his new shoes, until at last a woman wearing a uniform with a bunch of jangling keys hanging from her waist opened the door. "What it is? What brings you here?" she asked crossly.

Ion showed her the photograph and repeated his parents' names. "They may have been here for many years, they may even have died," he said in a voice that was suddenly no more than a whisper.

"They are not here. We have no one here of that name. Try elsewhere," she said, already closing the door.

"But where shall I go next? What am I to do?" shouted Ion desperately. "Tell me, please tell me."

"That's your business. Ask the guards at the gates," she added, relenting a little.

Walking away he thought, well at least I didn't cry.

The guards laughed when he asked them. "There are so many prisoners in this country and hundreds of prisons. It's like looking for a needle in a haystack. You should go home and forget all about it," the tallest said.

"Haven't you ever had a letter?" asked the other.

Ion shook his head. "Only a line once saying that they were alive," he said.

"They must be dead by now then. No one lasts long in prison," said the other with a brutal laugh.

Ion walked away from the prison and then sat down and wept. His tears made small holes in the snow while his feet froze in the pointed shoes. The sky grew grayer and grayer, and the sun fainter and fainter. And he thought of many things: how his whole life had been blighted because he had no parents, and now his grandmother might be dying almost alone. He remembered Christmas after Christmas without his parents and name-day after name-day, and he wept for how it might have been. He cried because of the cold and miserable prisoners who had spent years behind wire and would most likely die there. And he cried because he was all alone, and homesick to the marrow of his bones. After a time he opened the package of food Cristina had given him and ate what was inside. He thought, perhaps I should walk back to the capital, perhaps she will help me. Perhaps I will telephone her. But at that moment an old woman appeared with a bundle of sticks on her head. Leaning over him with a mouth full of rotting teeth she said, "You will freeze to death here. Come to my house. I have some hot soup on the stove."

So after a moment Ion stood up and followed her and went into her house, which was quite near and small, with an earth floor, and not much inside besides a table, three chairs, and a bed, with an icon and a cross hanging above it. She gave him soup and rough bread and asked, "What brings you here? You're only a lad to be on your own."

So he told her what had happened and when he had finished she said, "My father was taken away. He never returned. But my son will be here in the morning. He has a truck and will take you on to the next town; there's a prison there. But I do not think you will be lucky, I

have to say that. I must be honest with you."
She dried his clothes by the fire, which was in
the middle of the room.

She reminded Ion of his grandmother. Her
hair was arranged in the same way and there
was a pump outside and chickens that wan-
dered indoors as though they owned the place.
It was the same, but different because it wasn't
his village and his grandmother wasn't there.

6

Frozen Stiff

Ion woke early the next morning, but not as early as the old peasant woman, who plied him with goat's milk and mush.

"I like your clothes," she said. "It's not often one sees such clothes!"

Ion told her about the revolution, and then about Cristina, and when he had finished she sighed and said, "Oh, yes, we all know Cristina and the story of her poor son. First her husband went for a walk in the mountains and never returned. Then her son died. Such disaster, and to think that once her family owned all this valley and half the mountains as well. But they were taken away a long time ago. She could have gone to live abroad, but she stayed; she

61

wanted to change things. But no one can change them, or only God," and the old woman crossed herself.

"But there's been a revolution," Ion said and then told her about his relations in England, and how, like Cristina, he had nearly gone, but in the end had returned for the same reason. And so nearly an hour passed, and then came a banging on the door and in another minute the old woman's son stood before them. He had dark curly hair, a wild untrimmed mustache, and was broad-shouldered and roughly five feet tall. Ion's first thought was, he looks like a Gypsy, he'll be after my money. For in his village no one trusted Gypsies. So Ion stood up and put on his coat, and felt in his inside pocket to make sure that the money and photograph were still there. Then the old woman bade them both farewell while Ion groped in his pocket for money and gave her a few coins, which made her kiss his hand. No one had ever done that before. It's because I know Cristina and wear expensive clothes, he thought, following her son outside.

The truck was old, with worn tires and no windshield wipers. Rust had eaten into its wings and left them jagged, the license plate was held together by wire, and a headlight was smashed.

"She goes," said the old woman's son, who was called Josef, kicking the bumpers.

The mountains seemed nearer now and less formidable.

Josef used a starting handle to start the traction engine. "Righty ho, hop in. It's a fair old trip to the asylum. I hope we make it," he said.

"I thought we were going to a prison," Ion answered, settling himself inside the truck.

"It's the same thing, ain't no different. Anyone who opposes the government is mad, that's how it goes," replied Josef as they set off. "You must be insane to oppose such comforts, mustn't you? I mean, we have everything: new cars, plenty to eat. We're lucky, aren't we?"

It was then that Ion realized he was being sarcastic, and replied, "Of course," in a loud voice.

After ten minutes or so they stopped so that Josef could have a swig of brandy, "to keep out the cold," he said. And Ion had to admit it was very cold inside the truck, with no heating whatsoever.

Snow was falling silently outside. They had the mountain road to themselves. After another swig of brandy, Josef broke into rude songs and so they traveled for another hour, higher and higher into the mountains, the engine of the old truck struggling, the gears grinding, the worn tires slipping, so that twice Ion thought they were going over the edge of the road to certain death below. Josef's face was flushed now and his songs grew ruder and ruder and then quite suddenly the truck stopped altogether. "Overheating, that's what it is," said Josef, now so drunk he could hardly stand.

"What do we do now?" Ion asked.

"Wait for it to cool."

"How long will that be?"

"An hour or more." Josef emptied the brandy bottle down his throat as he spoke.

"Why are you going to the town?" Ion asked next.

"To see a woman and to do a bit of business," replied Josef in a drunken voice. "But you can go on if you like. You don't have to stay with me," he added. "Go on, beat it. Go. I'm going to have a sleep and there's only room for one in the cab." He smelled dreadful now, of unwashed body and drink. "Go. Get out," he shouted, growing more aggressive every passing second.

"All right. I'm going," said Ion in an aggrieved voice, making sure his money and the photograph were still in his pocket before he jumped out of the cab onto the hard-packed snow. And now as he walked on everything was very quiet, without even a bird to be seen. Later on Ion met a few vehicles, but they were all going in the wrong direction, and though the drivers looked at him curiously, they did not stop. His feet slipped and his hands froze, and before long there was an icicle on the end of his nose.

After a time Ion could see a town in the distance, but for ages it never seemed to grow any nearer, and the road wound round and round through the mountains without getting anywhere. Soon fear and hunger gnawed at Ion's stomach and he longed for Cristina, who would surely know the way and find him waterproof boots and dry gloves. Then he thought that if Stefan had telephoned Uncle Fanel in England as he'd asked him, everything might have been different, because everyone listened to people from the West, knowing their pockets were stuffed with dollars, sterling, and German marks. Dollars in particular could move mountains. Dollars would have found him a taxi and a driver; they would have bribed the prison guards and found his parents. But Stefan was afraid too; they were all afraid of the stupid President, who looked like a nobody.

It was like a disease, Ion thought scornfully, as he reached flat land at last. Now his legs were aching, and his feet were raw and frozen inside his shoes. He would have wept then if there had been anyone to see his tears, but everything was frozen, silent. Even the river he had reached was stilled by ice. So there was nothing Ion could do but go on or lie down in the snow and perish. And now snow was falling from a darkening sky and the flakes were growing larger every moment, thousands and thousands of them. I must go on, Ion told himself. I owe it to my grandmother. I must never give up. And he shouted at his legs, "One two, one two. March, will you." But they were tired and stiff and frozen and would only shuffle. Then at last he saw a street, parked cars, television antennas, but though his heart leaped with hope, his legs refused to run. They had never refused him before.

Dusk was descending now and Ion could see no sign of the asylum anywhere, just blinding snow. Then his eyes refused to focus properly and started to play tricks. Twice he thought he saw Cristina standing in the road ahead of him calling, "Follow me." But when he looked again she wasn't there. Then he saw his grandmother staggering toward him, but when he looked again the road was empty. Soon I will fall down like an old horse and never get up again, he thought; and then he saw his parents running toward him hand in hand, their faces wreathed in smiles. He tried to run to meet them but fell, and when he stood up again of course they were no longer there, just the empty snowy road. I'm going mad, he thought, and rubbed his eyes and banged his sides with stiff arms. Then he reached some wrought-iron gates, and his legs buckled under him and he sank into the snow completely exhausted and thought: this is the end, I've failed, and I will never see home again.

Soon after that a woman appeared who Ion thought was an angel. She helped him into a house that was like a dream, with television, fancy lights, a washing machine, a fridge, even a Christmas tree.

"Whoever are you?" the woman asked. "Why aren't you at home? You're frozen stiff. Are you a Gypsy?" Ion shook his head, while she took off his frozen clothes and rubbed his frozen feet. "Rub your hands together," she said. Then she gave him a hot drink. She was very matter-of-fact, not like any of the women he knew, who would have been all over him, crying to see the state he was in. All Ion could think of saying was, "Do you know Cristina? She once owned all this area, even the mountains."

"Oh, her, she's a troublemaker. And I can assure you she never owned this street," the woman said. And Ion saw that she was sharp-faced, with downy hair on her upper lip, and wore shiny shoes.

"I was with her in the revolution," Ion muttered.

"And that was a mistake," the woman said. "Oh, here's my husband. He'll sort you out."

And Ion thought, I should never have mentioned Cristina. They're enemies. But my heart aches for her. No one else is as good. She knows everything.

The woman's husband was a doctor. He made Ion sit in a chair and looked inside his mouth, then took his temperature. "Well, there's nothing wrong with you, except you're a bit exhausted," he said.

"I suppose he had better stay the night. We can hand him to the police in the morning," the woman said.

"I'm on my way to the asylum," Ion explained quickly. "I have to go there."

"How interesting. I work there," replied the doctor, smiling.

And then, of course, Ion felt faint with surprise. A minute later he had produced the photograph. "Do you know them? The name is Radu. Lucian and Tantza. I have come miles to find them," he said.

The doctor looked at the photograph with little interest. "There are hundreds of such people in the asylum. I personally look after a thousand of them and they all look the same to me, but I will take you there in the morning," he said after a moment. "Some are to be released. But the list has yet to be drawn up," he continued, without smiling.

"My parents were never mad," Ion replied boldly. "All they did was to hold money for someone else."

"Well, that was a mad thing to do, wasn't it?" the doctor asked. "No sane person would have done such a thing."

Later Ion heard the doctor and his wife talking about him. "He knows Cristina. And supposing he has head lice. I know his clothes look good, but he talks like a peasant," she said.

"We'll get rid of him first thing. I don't recognize his parents, but then it is a very old photograph. The name rings a bell, though . . . Radu, Radu. I know the name," the doctor said.

And now Ion's heart felt swollen with hope for his parents.

The doctor and his wife fed him in the kitchen, eating together in another room. Ion marveled at their belongings. Everything looked expensive. Later they locked him inside a room, saying, "The bed's made up. Go to sleep. We'll talk in the morning."

It was a very bare room because they had

hastily removed anything of value, fearing that he might steal it. The bed had a blanket and a comforter on it. The window was locked. They're afraid too, Ion thought. But of what? Not of me, surely? He could hear the television on in the next room. The President had been shot. There was still fighting in the capital. There was no mention of Cristina. Was she dead? Would he ever see her again? Ion was afraid of what would happen in the morning now. The police might lock him up, or worse still take him back to his village. How ashamed he would feel then! He did not want to sleep now, but it overcame him just the same when he was still fully dressed and sitting on the bed, trapped in the locked room.

7

Inside the Asylum

O<small>N WAKING</small> I<small>ON</small> thought he was in a prison cell. Then he remembered, and found that the door was still locked, the window locked and shuttered. I'm so near to my parents, he thought in anguish. I can't bear to be sent home and then start on this long journey all over again. During the night his feet had bled on the comforter, smudging it with blood.

Another minute and the police may be here, he thought next, for now he could hear the doctor and his wife moving about the house. He imagined himself handcuffed in a car. The long journey back, only to find his grandmother dead or dying; the village gone, just mounds where the houses had once stood. The cows unfed, the dogs lost. Stefan the only person left, even Mr. Ditescu moved, his books left rotting beneath the snow outside. Ion imagined everything he had ever loved destroyed. The police pushing him out of their police car, shouting, "You're home now, peasant boy."

He started banging on the locked door, shouting all the time, "Let me out, let me out. I haven't done anything wrong." Then he called the doctor and his wife every hateful name he knew, and some of them were very rude and some of them just plain stupid, and none of it did him any good. Then he started to feel like a wild animal suddenly caged and tore at the door with his hands. And he knew by the light coming through the cracks in the shutters that it was another day. And he thought, I've wasted too much time on the revolution, but what else could I have done?

Then he heard the doctor say, "Hang on, darling. I'll give him an injection. That will keep him quiet until the police arrive."

Ion was very frightened now, and fell silent. He imagined himself limp and helpless, writhing with pain. And he thought, so that's what they do in the asylum. That's how they make people mad. And now he was even more frightened. He broke into a sweat and his hands shook as, hoping for a miracle, he tried the door once more. But it was still locked, so he crawled under the bed and hid there, hoping that the doctor wouldn't hear the frantic beating of his heart.

The doctor filled a syringe. He looked very grave and reliable as quietly he entered the room, the sort of man you would trust with everything you had. He looked distinguished too in his well-made suit, with his silver-gray hair well brushed, his nails manicured, and his shoes polished. "Where are you, boy? I want to give you something. It's no good hiding. I want to help you find your parents," he said.

Ion wanted to shout, "Liar," but held his tongue and waited, like a cornered animal, every muscle ready to spring, every nerve tense, heart racing, while inside himself he prayed for strength.

The doctor picked up the comforter, shook it, and sighed when he saw the blood there. Ion waited, almost dizzy with suspense. Not too soon, he thought inside himself, bide your time. The doctor went to the window and sighed again. "I'm here to help you, you silly boy. I'm a doctor, I make people better," he explained in a soothing voice. "Soon you will be united with your parents."

Another second, and Ion leaped from under the bed, rushed through the door, and straight across the sitting room to the front door and, as he rushed, he prayed at the speed of an express train, "Let it be open, please, God, let it be open." And it was. So in a flash he was out in the street running for his life, not caring where he ran, just running on and on, away from the doctor and his wife, like a wild animal just escaped from captivity.

He ran without looking, and presently he collided with a moped. Dismounting, the young man riding it cried, "Are you all right? You ran straight into me. Have you no eyes in your head? You could have been killed." And he sounded both frightened and upset.

Ion sat up and looked around. There was no sign of the doctor, but a small crowd was beginning to collect. "I have to go to the asylum. I must hurry. I've come a long way," he gasped, standing up.

"I'm going that way too. Hop up behind me. I think this machine still goes," the young man said. "Sit tight."

"Why are you going there? Are you a doctor?" Ion asked suspiciously, knowing that he would never trust a doctor again.

The young man laughed. "I'm going because they are releasing people and my wife has been held there for months. She's coming home with me." And as he spoke, tears of joy ran down his face. He revved up the engine and they set off.

"My parents may be there. I don't know for certain, but I must look," Ion replied, and glanced behind him, to see whether the doctor was following. But the street was almost empty now. The small crowd had dispersed and a winter sun was shining down.

"When did you last see your parents?" asked the young man, who was called Dan.

"When I was two."

"That's a long time ago. They may even be dead. Have you thought of that?" Dan asked.

"Yes, a thousand times."

"It's really a prison," Dan said.

"I know. They make people mad there. I've just escaped from a doctor who wanted to make me mad," replied Ion, and told Dan what had happened. Of course, Dan didn't quite believe his story and Ion wasn't surprised when he thought about it, for even to himself it appeared extraordinary.

The asylum was in an old castle, with a cluster of asbestos huts nearby. Everything looked gray and forbidding, and all of it was surrounded by high walls with broken glass embedded in the top.

"This is it," announced Dan, dismounting from his moped. "I know where my darling wife is, but you had better go to the office and ask there. Good luck."

And now Ion's heart was fluttering inside him like a small captive bird. Then he thought, I must hurry or the wicked doctor will get there first and forbid their release, or have me arrested. He may even be there already. And so Ion rushed up the steps and, pushing open a heavy door, was suddenly in a hall, where all the doors were locked, and only a pathetic gray-haired woman was there on her knees washing the stone floor.

"I'm looking for someone," Ion said. "I need help."

She gazed at him with the eyes of a frightened animal and went on wiping the floor, the same piece over and over again. Then she looked at him and asked, "Am I doing all right? I am, aren't I?" And her eyes were the appealing eyes of a child in an old demented face.

Ion felt like weeping as he answered, "Yes, it's excellent."

And she smiled at him and went on wiping the same piece of floor while Ion's heart grew colder and colder inside him. He thought, supposing my mother is the same? Supposing she's mad? Supposing she doesn't recognize me? Oh, God, help me, please God.

He found a bell and pushed on it, and after a few minutes, which seemed like hours, a woman in a white coat appeared and asked sharply, "Yes, what is it? What do you want?"

"I want my parents," Ion replied, and it seemed the most basic and yet the most complicated thing he had ever said.

"Name, please," she replied, looking at him with hate in her eyes, but with something else there too, which could have been a glimmer, just a tiny glimmer of fear. It filled Ion with sudden hope as he produced the photograph and showed it to her. He told her their names and she stared at the photograph before she asked, "Was it taken a long time ago?"

"Yes." Ion could hardly speak now, so great was his feeling of suspense. Then he thought, why is she taking so long? Why doesn't she speak? "Please hurry. I have a long way to go," he said. "Please, honorable doctor, I implore you." And he looked over his shoulder to see whether the wicked doctor had arrived, but there was still no sign of him.

"Stay here," the woman said after another long moment had passed. "There are many prisoners in our country. You will be lucky if you find them here."

"I know, but I want them now. I can't wait, can't you understand?" cried Ion, his mind in agony.

"I said wait, and I mean wait," the woman replied, going back the way she had come, locking the door after her.

"Am I doing all right?" asked the old scarecrow of a woman wiping the floor.

"Very well indeed," Ion said while his heart

seemed to be breaking inside him and tears ran down his face.

"I am, aren't I?"

"Yes."

"I was young once, you know, and very pretty."

"I'm sure you were," Ion replied, his eyes on the doors while his legs felt weak beneath him, and his mind remained in agony.

"Nobody leaves here alive, you know," said the old woman.

"I know. But there's been a revolution," Ion replied.

And then the other woman came back and beckoned to him saying, "Follow me. They're here and on the list to go. We have orders to release nearly everyone. You're in luck this time."

"You know them then? They're really here?" cried Ion, unable to believe his ears, wanting everything confirmed. "You're not mistaken?"

"No. They're getting changed now. Clothes have been delivered from France. Of course, we're going to lose our jobs," she said. And Ion, thinking of the doctor, asked, "All of you?"

"I think so."

"Even the doctors?"

"Yes, they're arresting them now," she said. "Go straight ahead. Don't loiter."

Then Ion was running along a corridor where a group of people were waiting at the end and, as he ran, he shouted, "Mother, Father, it's me—your son Ion. There's been a revolution and I'm taking you home." And as he ran more tears fell down his face in an unstoppable flood.

8

"I Can't Believe It"

Bᴜᴛ ᴛʜᴇʏ ᴡᴇʀᴇɴ'ᴛ there. Ion stopped, dizzy with disappointment. The exhausted faces of strangers stared at him, and he felt the sickness of disappointment growing in his stomach. He looked again at the faces gazing at him hollow-eyed. "We're so sorry," one muttered, while another one said, "Don't stop searching," and a third muttered through toothless gums, "Perhaps they've passed away."

And all Ion could think was, she said they were here, she knew their names, and so did the doctor. Then he thought that the doctor might have telephoned the hospital and said, "Don't let the Radus go free. These are my express orders." And he felt a fresh rush of tears in his eyes, and a new kind of hate rising inside of him.

Then a tired woman appeared and asked, "Are you looking for someone?" She was a foreigner, Ion could sense it, or at least she had lived abroad for many years. His heart warmed to her. He got out the photograph and showed it to her.

"Stay with me," she said. "They won't look like they did then, of course. I can see it was taken a long time ago. But I will help you."

He wanted to kiss her hand, but she was already hurrying ahead of him, her mind set on finding them, her smart shoes clattering along an endless, ill-smelling corridor without windows, lit only by a faint electric bulb. "Torture chambers," she said once, stopping to point at a thick, barred door. They reached the outside again, where more people waited in the snow with resigned, empty faces like animals penned without hope, far from home. But Ion's parents were not there either.

Ion could see now that the woman had long,

glossy hair and high cheekbones. Glancing at him, she said, "I fled this country years ago. But it has always been in my heart, so I had to come back to help. But now I'm here, I'm afraid I'm too late."

"Nobody can be too late," replied Ion after a moment.

They entered the building by another door. "I won't let you down. France has sent me to see that justice is done," the woman said. "And now I wonder whether anyone here understands the word *justice*. Do you?"

"I think so," replied Ion, but wasn't sure. And then he saw them sitting on chairs in a sort of hall, and he knew them at once, and that surprised him, for now there was absolutely no doubt in his mind as he ran forward once again, crying, "I am your son, Ion. Do you remember me? I've come to take you home."

They looked much older and there was a terrible, unbearable silence before Ion was in his mother's arms with her tears falling into his hair. Next she raised his face and looked at it.

"I thought I would never see this day. How you have grown and I have missed it all," she cried. Then he turned to his father, whose head was shaven, his mustache gone. He tried to pick up Ion as he had long ago, but was not strong enough, so he embraced him instead. He smelled of prison soap and prison clothes.

"We've been separated so long," his mother said. "How have you managed all these years? I've thought of you so often. I wrote so many letters, night after night. I started the moment they stopped torturing me, the moment I had a chance, but I never had an answer."

"But we never had a letter from you, not one. Only a line saying you were still alive, nothing else. If we'd had a letter, it would have changed everything," Ion cried.

"Oh, no, and so many wasted years," said his mother as a warden brought them clothes, saying, "Get dressed. You are free to go. These are a gift from France."

Ion waited for them outside, where the air felt better. Everywhere families were uniting.

Old men were singing old songs in croaky voices, while others choked over foreign cigarettes. Other people were laughing and shouting to one another, "We're free, we're going home. Thank God."

Then his parents reappeared and his father said, "They've given me some money." And his voice was full of wonder.

"It seems like a dream," his mother said. "And I'm so afraid it won't last. That it's just one more trick."

His father had a front tooth missing. He was wearing a pair of French shoes on his large feet and a dark suit and a gray cap. Made for a fatter person, the clothes hung on him. Ion's mother was wearing a black skirt, a long sweater, a large coat, and a woolly hat. They were probably not the sort of clothes she had ever worn before, but the woolly hat suited her, thought Ion, and hid her thinning hair.

They found a waiting bus and climbed into it. "It will take us to the capital," his father said.

Ion told them about Uncle Fanel's visit and how he had wanted him to go to England.

"And how is my brother?" asked Ion's father as the bus started.

"All right." We are talking like strangers. We should be talking warmly, we should be laughing, Ion told himself.

But the other passengers were the same; thunderstruck, they stared out the bus windows, wondering whether they were living a dream, or whether it was just a ploy to move them without trouble, or a day out arranged by the foreigners.

"Is it a long way home?" his mother asked after a time.

"Miles, but the village is almost the same as you remember it—just a few deaths and a few births. There's only one cow left; they took the others to the cooperative farm. I just hope she isn't dry." And now Ion felt at least fifteen and it seemed years since he had left his village, a whole life away.

"What about my mother?" his father asked as

the bus wound its way through the mountains, wheezing and grunting like a worn-out old horse.

"Old and ill. She should be in a hospital, but they don't bother with old people anymore. I think they want them to die," Ion replied.

"Or a bribe," his father said. "They'll do anything for money."

Ion wished he didn't feel so old now. He wished he was a child again. He wished he could put the clock back ten years; it didn't seem much to ask. Most of all, he wished he had started searching for his parents long ago; but they had all been so frightened and, at that time, it was almost normal for people to disappear, never to be heard of again.

At last they reached the capital. It was almost night now, but the streets were still full of cheering crowds waving flags and singing the old anthem. Ion's parents watched them like nervous animals, wondering why they were allowed to behave in such a manner, while Ion could not help looking for Cristina, longing to tell her that he had succeeded and was on his way home.

"We'll go to the station," he told his parents. "I'll find the way. This is the revolution." They took a tram to the station, and it was free; because of the revolution everything was free that day. Walking down a street to the station, they saw candles flickering where people had died and small bunches of flowers wilting in the cold. And all the time Ion was still looking for Cristina. Then they came upon a truck distributing food, and Ion called out, "These two people are just out of prison. They are starving."

The drivers handed them small parcels. "There are vitamins inside too," they said in French.

Ion thanked them in their own language, which he had learned at school. His mother held on to his arm. When they reached the station, it was full of more cheering people. They sat on a bench and opened the parcels. Inside were chocolate, vitamin pills, small tins of meat, and powdered milk. And best of all, coffee. Ion's parents hadn't seen such things in years and wept, their tears running down their tired faces. Ion looked away, embarrassed, thinking that grown-ups shouldn't cry, especially men. He ate the chocolate as he stared up the line. The train was expected in twenty minutes. Once again they had not been allowed to pay for their tickets. "Today everything is free because we are free," the man in the ticket office had said, smiling jubilantly.

So they waited on the cold platform, which was covered with wet slush, and Ion could feel himself unwinding, his body suddenly limp with relief because he had achieved what he had set out to do. I can't be an orphan now, he thought, not ever. And I won't have to look after the cow and the geese and the chickens ever again, not all the time. Not as I have before. Mother will wash my clothes. Father will chop the wood. He looked at his parents, who were talking together in low voices, as though even the station might have bugging devices that would record everything they said and maybe send them back to prison. They looked frightened even now, sitting together in their ill-fitting clothes. The suit certainly didn't fit his father. His mother was far too thin for her outfit too and looked like a clotheshorse. They sat and whispered and nibbled at their chocolate, whereas Ion had already eaten his.

There were drunk men singing. There were young women walking up and down the platform arm in arm. Someone handed his parents a packet of cigarettes, which they accepted hungrily, but they had no matches to light them. Someone else gave them a light and they drew on the cigarettes like thirsty animals drinking at a water trough.

Ion paced the platform, for now he was imagining the village gone, his grandmother too. He was imagining the bulldozers far away, their terrible deed done just minutes before orders were changed and the revolution took over. He was thinking that Mr. Ditescu had once told him that "too late" were the saddest words he knew. At that time he had not understood what Mr. Ditescu meant, but he knew now as he paced the platform, his sore feet forgotten, his mind saying, "Hurry, train, hurry. Please, God, hurry."

It came at last, a huge train with the national flag stuck on the front. They clambered in.

"I can't believe it. I just can't believe it. You've been so good to us, Ion, coming all this way, and still so young," his mother said.

"It was nothing. I was scared, of course, at times, but it was all right," Ion answered, wishing that he'd had time to say good-bye to Cristina properly, wondering whether the wounded young man was dead, then searching for the map she had given him and finding it gone. So I've lost her address, he thought bitterly, and may never see her again.

The train drew out of the capital. Ion leaned out of the window for one last look at the station, half hoping to see Cristina there, her gun over her shoulder, her fair hair shining bright. But there was no sign of her, just people waving good-bye to friends and relatives. It was the first time he had traveled anywhere outside the village with his parents, who still sat close together talking quietly to one another, looking nervously around from time to time as though the secret police might suddenly appear to say that it was all a terrible mistake, that the revolution was over and they must go back to their cells for another ten years.

"You're free now, forever," Ion said, sitting down next to his mother. "And we're going home. Everyone will be there to meet you. There will be a celebration, just wait and see." But, of course, he couldn't be certain, because nothing in life is certain; he had learned that during the last few days and it would stay with him for the rest of his life.

Slowly they left the station behind, and now the countryside was clad in snow, the houses thatched with it, the trees bent beneath it. In the distance were mountains; maybe other, happier lands, thought Ion. But at least his parents had survived and were on their way home, and was there anything better than that, than going home?

His mother was dozing now. They had put out their cigarettes. His father had his hands folded on his knees. He looked at Ion and smiled. "Sit by me. Let us talk. You are my son, after all," he said.

But soon after that, exhausted, they too slept. Ion dreamed that he was with Cristina; she was running along a long tunnel and again he couldn't keep up. Laughing, she called, "At the end of the tunnel, there's freedom. Run faster or you'll never reach it." She held out her arms to him and they were full of bright yellow bananas.

When he awakened they were drawing into Augusta station and it was pitch dark. His father shook his mother awake. Ion started to pray, "Please, God, let the village still be there and Grandmother still alive," but only in his head, because he didn't want people to know he was praying.

Soon he could see that Party Headquarters

was no more than a blackened shell. The air smelled of burned carpet when they stepped out onto the platform, which was in semi-darkness, and there was still smoke rising from the black ruins.

There was a cab horse sagging between his shafts outside the station. Ion's father took one look at him and said, "He'll never make the village."

There were no taxis, and Ion thought that was typical of life. When they had the money there were no taxis, but when they had no money there were plenty. Snow was beginning to fall. His mother was pointing to huge apartment buildings in the distance. "They're new," she said. "Who lives there?"

"People, just people," replied Ion quickly, not wishing to dishearten her too soon.

Their shoes were unsuitable for snow. It seeped inside, soaking their thin socks. Ion fell to wondering how his grandmother would greet them. Would she have the strength to welcome them, to get out of bed, even? He kept scanning the distance to see whether the rooftops of the village were still there. It seemed years since he had taken his leave, yet it had only been a few days. He felt much older. He felt as though he would never be frightened of anything again. He wanted to run as they drew nearer to the village, but his father was holding up his mother now, talking to her gently.

The sky had cleared; their way was lit by the moon and the stars. And now everything smelled different. It smelled of the countryside, of woodsmoke and cow muck. Ion knew each turn in the road now; his eyes were searching for rooftops. He felt sick inside. His throat felt dry with suspense. If the village was razed to the ground there would be nowhere for them to go, no apartment allotted to his parents, no grandmother to welcome them—for in such circumstances she would surely be dead. He craned his neck and stood on tiptoe, but now all he could see were the apartment blocks, tall and gaunt. But there were no lights on in them, not even the glimmer of a candle. And now he could hear the village dogs barking as they always did at night-fall. He could hear the call of a fox and smell the slow, turgid river half frozen under the bridge.

His mother had stopped. "What are those buildings? They look like a prison," she cried, staring at the almost-finished apartments, which stood bare and strange in the moonlight, so much higher than the village. They didn't belong, they would never belong, even a fool could see that.

"They are for people from outside," replied Ion quickly, almost running now, his heart racing with suspense, imagining a ruin, seeing his mother's tears falling on the snow. The cow would be gone, the geese penned up somewhere. The yard dogs soon to be destroyed; the chick-ens given away. Then he saw the old familiar skyline, the roofs he knew so well still there. He was swamped with sudden, indescribable joy and relief. He turned to his parents and cried, "Hurry, we're nearly home. And it's still there." He started to run while they moved their tired legs a little faster, slipping and skidding in their unsuitable French shoes. Then he saw that there was a light on in Mr. Ditescu's house, and it seemed to welcome him home, to be saying, "So you made it after all." And he wanted to shout and cheer, to leap in the air and cry, "I've found them. They're still alive. And everything's going to be all right."

The bulldozers were no longer parked on the far side of the village. Seeing that made Ion feel as though yet another cloud had been lifted from his heart. And then, seizing his mother's arm, he cried, "Look, it's just the same, nothing's changed." Then he was running ahead, then stopping to wait, stamping his tired feet like an impatient horse. I've succeeded, we're home, he thought again and again, and it was like a dream come true. He would never feel like an orphan again. Never be made to join the secret police. He was free. And now he understood why the people shouted freedom so loudly. It was the greatest thing on earth— "Freedom." His parents still didn't understand that. There was fear still written plainly on their faces. He could see it even in the moon-light. They were afraid to believe what was happening before their very eyes. They were afraid to be happy.

A light was on in the house. The yard dogs appeared in the moonlight to lick Ion's hands in welcome. The cow-house door was latched shut, and he could hear the geese talking to one another quietly, as they do at nighttime.

"Do you remember it, Father?" he cried. "Can you hear the geese talking?"

"Yes, of course, I can." His father was actually wiping tears from his eyes as Ion unlatched the familiar gate.

"We're back. My parents are here and there's been a revolution. We're free," he cried.

He had dreamed so long of this moment. He had given up hope time and time again. He had nearly gone away and abandoned his parents forever. So now he wanted to shout to the whole world, "It's happened. Dreams do come true."

Soon people woke up and emerged from their

homes to shake his father's hand and to kiss his mother's. The old ones crossed themselves and said, "Thanks be to God."

"But we have nothing to give, nothing," cried old Roxana, who was the oldest woman in the village, with teeth covered with aluminum. "Nothing."

So there was to be no banquet, for you cannot have one without food. Maria threw her arms around Ion. "So you made it. Well done," she cried.

And now he was suddenly very tired. "How is Grandma?" he asked.

"Near to her end," a woman said. "You are just in time." She crossed herself as she spoke, while suddenly the moon appeared again and shone bright on the old home that Ion's parents had built with their own hands so long ago.

9

Kill the Gander

THE VILLAGERS RETURNED to their beds. Ion and his parents smelled the old familiar smell. They saw the familiar rugs that his English cousins had once called "carpets" hanging on the wall. There was a light in the house. A faint light, but then, all the lights were faint at this hour. Ion ran toward it. His grandmother was there. Nina sat beside her. "She's still alive. I'm glad you're back in time. Shall I send for the priest?" she asked, as though Ion was a grown man and knew such things. Then Nina saw his parents, and leaping to her feet, embraced them both. And Grandmother seemed to rally then, and held out her arms to Ion's father, saying, "My son, my son."

"So the revolution is true. I know the bull-dozers have left. But is it true?" asked Maria.

"Yes. All true," Ion said, taking off his shoes, walking barefoot toward the cellar in search of food. He was trying to come to terms with the welcome, which seemed so sober and sad, not at all as he had expected. He was trying not to cry, because nothing was as he had expected it to be. After being in the capital, everything seemed poor and simple, as though he was seeing it all for the first time as it really was.

His mother was kneeling beside Grandma's bed now, trying to hear what she was saying. His father was pacing the room saying, "We must get her to the hospital. Is there anyone in the village with a car?"

"Only the secret policeman," Ion replied.

"He's not one anymore. They have been abolished. Do I know him? Who is this fellow?" his father asked.

"I will fetch him," Ion said.

His mother wound a scarf round his neck. She looked at his hard, callused hands and sighed. His grandma's breathing was too fast now, even Ion knew that, too fast and too loud. It followed him out the door, down the rough road to Stefan's door. Ion felt brave now; he wasn't frightened of secret policemen anymore, because this time it was a real revolution, not like the previous one, which had drowned in a sea of promises and many deaths. He banged on Stefan's door and the ex-secret policeman came to it cautiously, in his nightshirt, no doubt thinking that it was his turn to be arrested.

"We need your help. We need a car. Grandma needs to go to the hospital." Ion wasn't afraid to tell the truth now. He thought that Stefan was like a bear with his teeth pulled out—he couldn't hurt him or his parents ever again.

"So I'm not an orphan after all," Ion continued. "And we need your car. Straight away, please."

Stefan couldn't refuse, for he needed people to think well of him now before it was too late. He had to make amends. Besides, he had only been a secret policeman because of the rewards;

his heart had never been in it. His mind had wanted things and ignored the call from his heart. It had wanted a car and good food and so, against his better judgment, he had become a policeman.

So presently, when he was dressed, he uncovered his car, which was really quite old, and drove Ion down the road. "They may not take her in. They don't like the old in the hospital. They have so few nurses. This country doesn't like the old or the very young—they're too much trouble," Stefan said, changing gear.

"Not anymore," Ion replied. "They've changed." But watching his grandmother being carried out of the house wrapped in blankets and her quilt, he had to admit the village had not really changed at all, not yet. The old lady kept asking questions in a querulous voice. "Where are you taking me now?" she asked. "And who will look after the house with Ion gone?"

"I'm here, look, Grandma!" Ion cried. But the

next moment she had forgotten him and was asking the same questions again.

Ion went with his father, squeezed into the back of the car, which skidded so on the unplowed road that twice they nearly left it altogether. The moon had vanished. And now it seemed the longest day of Ion's life.

When they reached the hospital, Stefan found a stretcher. Then they carried the old lady inside. Nothing was showing above the quilt now besides her old eyes. The wards were crowded with beds and many of the occupants were children.

Ion's father had taken over now, and rushed around the hospital, his clothes flapping on his emaciated body, seeking help for his mother. A bed was found for her, and a doctor fetched, who was so tired that he could hardly put two words together.

"I don't care if she is in her seventies, I still want her cared for, you understand? And please remember I have a brother in the West, who will raise the matter if she's not treated as she should be," shouted Ion's father.

So at last Grandma lay in bed between clean sheets. The doctor took her pulse and listened to her chest while Ion dozed in a chair. Soon after that they set off for home again.

"Is she going to live?" Ion asked.

"I doubt it. She needs antibiotics. And that's only given to officials and the like, not to the elderly," his father replied.

Stefan's hands were clean and manicured on the steering wheel. He was wearing a shirt from the West, perhaps from London, and smart trousers and good shoes and a jacket that fitted. He looked well-clothed and well-fed and there were wrinkles of fat at the back of his neck. Ion couldn't help admiring him now, though he wanted to hate him. He was no longer a peasant. He was so cool and clean and competent, and he knew his way around.

"Your uncle may arrive uninvited, who knows?" he asked with a laugh.

After that Ion slept so soundly that when

they reached home his father helped him to bed, and when he awakened again the cocks were crowing outside and it was like any other morning, except that his parents were back and his grandmother in a hospital. The cow still needed milking, the geese letting out, the chickens feeding. The dogs, which had roamed free all night, must be shut in the yard. Water must be fetched from the pump.

Ion stumbled outside and washed under the pump. His father was already up, and said, "The place is empty of food. How long has it been like this?"

"A long time. But there is maize in the cellar and in a minute I'll milk the cow and you can have fresh milk," Ion said.

He was so tired that now it was only habit that kept him going, for he could have looked after the animals blindfolded. But now he didn't want to go on looking after them. He wanted a car like Stefan, and clean hands. He was beginning to think that being a secret policeman had its compensations. He thought too that nothing was changing fast enough; he had found his parents, brought them home, and here he was still milking the cow, as he had every day for years. And in spite of the revolution, the cellar was still almost empty of food, the chickens thin, the village poor.

He fetched a pail and a stool and started to milk, and realized that nothing was as he had hoped. Though his grandmother was in the hospital, she would not have the medicine that might save her and so would die just the same, between clean sheets, it is true, with food and maybe a doctor in attendance. The capital seemed far away now, the last few days as distant as the moon, Ion thought, getting up from under the cow's flank to strain the milk. The only thing saved was the village, he thought, watching the meager milk dripping into a jug. The last few days he had been on a high, anything had seemed possible—death, success, failure, prison. Now he was home, he was back in the same old routine, another sort of prison, he thought angrily, taking the milk to the house.

It was snowing again and it might go on for days. Last year he had dug the house out twice. This time surely his father would do it? Perhaps he might even have a chance to throw snowballs and toboggan on a rough, homemade sled on the hill with other children.

Soon Ion's father was pacing up and down the house shouting, "This place is falling down. Can't you see that, Ion? And the cow is nearly dry and there's only half a sack of maize in the cellar. What have you been doing all these years? How am I to feed your mother, who is so weak this morning that she can hardly stand?"

"There's only been me and Grandma and I've had to go to school. I could have gone away to England and deserted her, but I didn't," Ion said, his heart sinking into his blistered feet. "You don't know how hard it's been, Father. Ask the other villagers, go on, ask them."

"Stefan's done all right."

"He's been a secret policeman, that's why."

"While I was in prison I watched television. It was full of the achievements of this country.

It showed great harvests, irrigation schemes, peasants dancing. I thought when I came out one day, there would be plenty, and what do I find? Nothing," cried Ion's father in an anguished voice.

Then he sat in a chair with his head in his hands and wept, and Ion, who had lived with such things for a long time, didn't know what to say. Finally he said, "I'll make some mush for Mother. I know how to do it. Soon it will be summer and the grapes will be ready for picking and we'll all be happy again."

But he knew it wouldn't be like that, for summer was a long time away. He thought, Father is right, I should have dug the garden. I should have grown carrots and buried them in the earth ready for the long winter months. I should have planted potatoes and let the plums dry in the sun until they became prunes, and pickled the walnuts. I should have done what Grandma did before she became old and feeble. Now Ion felt horribly guilty; then he remembered that the geese were still there, and though he loved them he said, "We can kill a goose, Father. We still have five." Then he took a bowl of thick golden mush that he had made out of the ground maize in the cellar to his mother, who was still in bed, lying quietly and seeming lost under a pile of quilts and old coats.

His father's voice followed him. "At least we had food in prison, not much, it's true, but something," he said.

Then his mother cried, "He doesn't mean it, Ion. He doesn't know what he's saying. I can see these years have been hard for you too. I can see it on your hands and written on your face. Don't blame yourself. You've done your best and without you we would have nothing."

Ion was trying not to cry, because soon he would be thirteen, and boys don't cry anyway. How often his grandmother had said that to him, wiping his tears away.

The snow had stopped falling; the sun had come out. Ion yearned for spring now, for the first leaves on the tall trees, for the vines to turn green again, for the blossoms to burst forth in a great galaxy of color on the fruit trees, for tortoises and lizards in the vineyards, for hope to come back to them all.

Ion's father went down the road to borrow a radio. Soon they sat listening to it, hearing gunfire and cheers, singing and laughter. New people were in control and they were saying what they liked at last, and the President was dead and buried. The news was thrilling and shocking at the same time because once, a long time ago, they had loved the President. It was only later, when he had become a monster, that they had hated him.

All political prisoners were now free and they learned that the secret police were being hunted down. Ion imagined Stefan being hunted. Would he be gunned down or would he go quietly in handcuffs? And who would have his car? Suddenly Ion didn't want him arrested, for now he understood why he had become a secret policeman. He had yearned for a better life, and perhaps maybe he hadn't been such a bad policeman after all. Then Ion wondered whether he had hidden his uniform yet. He imagined Stefan burying it, his neat manicured hands dirty. He would have no job now; he would be like the rest of them. Maybe he would become a taxi driver, Ion decided next, for it was impossible to imagine Stefan working in the hot fields, toiling from dawn to sunset. He was too clever for that; he would always be one jump ahead of the rest of them.

"Which goose shall I kill, then?" asked his father, suddenly beside him.

"You're going to do it, then?" Ion asked sadly.

"Well, we must eat, mustn't we?" his father said.

Ion went out and looked at the geese and now they were part of him; each one was different, and they knew him as a friend.

"Kill the gander," he said at last.

"I can't do that. If I kill the gander, we won't have any more goslings. Use your brain, Ion," cried his father.

Fortunately at that moment Mr. Ditescu came down the road and stopped to greet his father. "You have a wonderful son, Lucian. You should be proud of him," he said.

"Come in and have a drink. I have found a little brandy," replied Ion's father. And so the goose was saved.

Ion recognized the brandy; it was the same brandy his grandmother had kept for accidents and emergencies. It was all they had left.

"And he succeeded. He's a brave lad," continued Mr. Ditescu, still talking about Ion, in his clipped educated voice. And he put his arm on Ion's shoulder and said, "I congratulate you. One day you must visit me and tell me all about it. Don't forget."

Then his father and Mr. Ditescu sat drinking brandy and talking about the revolution, and now the snow was melting outside, the icicles on the trees dripping, the ice breaking around the edges of the little river, which was never really clean because dead animals and refuse were thrown into it.

And now, without his grandmother, Ion's day

seemed without order. He missed her calling to him: "Where are you, Ion? What are you doing now? Bring me a little glass of something, will you?" Though it had sometimes been tiresome, he had grown used to her ways.

Mr. Ditescu was sitting with his mother now, his graying mustache drooping. He was offering her books to while away the time, a game of chess, dominoes perhaps? But she had never read books, though she could write. In her day, girls in the village didn't think much about education. They thought about getting married.

Later Mr. Ditescu talked to Ion. He said, "Don't give up, Ion. Things can get no worse, only better. That is life."

"I think we are going to starve to death, Mr. Ditescu, that's what I think," Ion said. "We are so far away from the capital, people will forget about us. I know now, Mr. Ditescu, that I should never have brought my parents home. We should have stayed in the capital. But I was thinking of my grandmother and of the cow and the geese and the chickens."

"Things will get better. I have told your

father to fetch his cows home from the cooperative farm, that will make a difference," Mr. Ditescu said. "And you will be given back the land they took from you."

Ion hoped that his father would milk the extra cows, for he had no wish to milk three cows every morning.

"You should have received payment for them, but the manager was a scoundrel," Mr. Ditescu said before taking his leave, silently and thoughtfully, like an official of a good government, thought Ion. And now Ion's heart was yearning for the capital, for an apartment with a bathroom and water that rushed out of the tap instead of needing to be fetched from the pump, and then heated. He wished he hadn't lost Cristina's address.

"How is your grandmother, Ion?" called Mr. Ditescu as he reached the gate.

"We don't know. How can we know without a telephone?" asked Ion.

"Ask Stefan to ring for you; he has one," replied Mr. Ditescu.

Then Ion thought that there was no justice in the world, if a man who had been wicked for as long as Stefan, who had lived well by reporting people to the authorities, acquired all he wanted while the rest of the village starved. He felt that there was no point in being honest, rather that one should live by one's wits. But even as he thought it, he could see Vasile, who was reputed to have a wooden leg, hobbling toward him calling, "They've come. They are driving down the road. God be praised, they're here." He looked demented and half wild with excitement.

And now Ion could hear a horn, and suddenly he knew who it was and ran into the house, calling, "It's Uncle Fanel. He's come. He's here. He's come to help." Then he was running outside again, waving his thin arms, while his mother left her bed and, pulling an old coat over herself, followed Ion outside. A van was coming down the road with Uncle Fanel at the wheel, hooting and waving out the window, his face red with excitement. And sitting beside him was Donald, the eldest of his children.

Uncle Fanel yelled out the window, "What a journey it's been! I thought I would never make it. How's Mother? I've brought medicines for her and food for the whole village, as much as I could fit in, and clothes too, clothes for everyone." And Ion saw that the van was flying the Union Jack and now, as all the villagers started appearing like phantoms, it seemed to him that this was the greatest moment of his entire life. How did he know we needed him? he thought. It's a miracle. It must be.

10

As Strong as an Ox

EVERYONE SEEMED TO be embracing everyone else. Wine was fetched from inside the van. Glasses appeared as though by magic. No one was left out. Biscuits and cakes were passed round—such cakes, no one had ever tasted the like before!

"We'll have a feast tomorrow," announced Uncle Fanel. "But before that I must see my mother, that is the first priority." He and Donald looked so clean and healthy compared to the villagers that they might have come from another world, thought Ion. Their clothes were clean and new; their hair washed and shining; they wore beautiful gloves and thick socks, and Fanel had Western cigarettes and a silver case to keep them in. Never had Ion felt so poor and shabby; as for his mother, she looked like a walking ghost.

"I think you are only just in time, for the cellar is bare and I was about to kill a goose," his father said.

"I've brought you a suit, but it will be too big, everything will be. You've all grown so thin," complained Uncle Fanel.

"And Ion hasn't grown at all," said Donald in English, which no one but his father understood.

"But at least the President's dead," said Fanel. "Now what about my mother? I've brought antibiotics, penicillin I think."

"But how did you know she needed it?" Ion's father looked surprised.

"Stefan rang me nearly a week ago. Then the revolution happened. I was going to fly, but the airport has been closed for days now, so I borrowed this van, and the people have filled it with things! Why, I've even brought things for the hospital. And we've been traveling day and night, sleeping when we can. And, well, we're here at last, as you can see. Now let's see my mother," he finished.

No one noticed that it was snowing, or if they did it no longer mattered. Uncle Fanel was handing out food and cigarettes now as though he was Father Christmas, while Donald looked round with dismay on his face, having never seen people so gaunt and ill before, like walking skeletons, he would say later—like people appearing from hell, he would add. And all looking the same, all gray with eyes staring out of thin, uniform faces.

So Stefan did as I asked, Ion thought. He changed his mind.

Then, tired as he was, Uncle Fanel turned the van and he and Donald sat in the front while Ion and his father squeezed into the back.

"This is a miracle," Ion's father said. "You are only just in time, I should think. The old lady was almost dead when we took her in and we haven't heard since. Thank God for Stefan."

"You could have used Stefan more," replied Uncle Fanel.

"In spite of his good deed, people say he was a secret policeman and one's still afraid," replied Ion's father with a sigh. "We are all still afraid. One never knows what may yet happen. I don't think I shall ever feel safe again."

"You can travel freely now, or so I've heard," replied Uncle Fanel. "I'll buy you plane tickets and you can come to us in England, and grow well again."

"Not as beggars. We won't come as beggars," cried Ion's father, who at heart was a proud man. "We won't come asking for charity."

They had reached the hospital. Uncle Fanel was first out. His energy was amazing. He strode into the hospital like a conqueror. He was afraid of nobody. There was a guard at the door, a young soldier who asked who they were.

"Who do you think I am? I'm Fanel Radu from England and I've come to see my mother," he cried.

Donald, who hated hospitals, and this one most of all, followed more slowly, thinking that in England they would have come with flowers and chocolates. The floors would be shiny and there would be nurses bustling about in starched aprons and smiling faces. But here there were large women in overalls with no laughter on their faces. The iron beds in the long, bare wards were close together, with hardly a foot between them. The electric light was dim because of the shortage of electricity. But now Uncle Fanel had found a doctor, a weary-looking man with black hair and sad brown eyes.

"I'm Fanel Radu." Ion watched his uncle take the doctor's arm. His father was completely overshadowed by his brother and looked like a scarecrow beside him. "I've brought this bottle of medicine for my mother. It is penicillin," said Uncle Fanel as though the doctor was an imbecile. "She's to have it three times a day. Is that clear?"

"I have more than two hundred patients to deal with, but I will see she has it," the doctor replied.

"I know you are overworked. Because of this I have brought you the best coffee money can buy, and I have dollars too," said Uncle Fanel. "And more medicines outside in the van—disposable syringes, antibiotics. I've brought them for this hospital and I don't want them sold on the black market. Do you understand?"

He was talking to the doctor as though he was a child, thought Ion. But now they were moving toward his grandmother. "Her heart is as strong as an ox, and her blood pressure is steady. The penicillin should take care of everything else," the doctor explained.

She was much worse, even Ion could see that. Without penicillin she would have died within twenty-four hours. Like Donald, he hated the hospital and didn't trust the doctor. A bottle of penicillin could be worth a fortune, for dying people would pay their last penny for it. Uncle Fanel didn't trust the doctor either, for the next moment he was saying, "I shall be back tomorrow and I expect the old

lady to have improved; there will be more coffee if she has, and I don't mind what you do
with it."

Then Fanel was talking to his mother, who
understood little and barely recognized him.

Quite soon the doctor said, "She must rest
now. Any conversation tires her. I will see she
has your medicine."

"He's a crook," said Uncle Fanel as they
returned to the van. "A damned awful crook.
We'll have to watch him."

"The whole country is corrupt, it's been the
only way to live. It's been a jungle. I see that
now," said Ion's father.

"I'll take some food for her tomorrow, real
food, not offal and thin soup made out of chickens' feet," said Uncle Fanel.

Ion wished he had stayed behind with his
mother, who was at home preparing a meal for
them, trying to open a can of baked beans with
an ancient can opener. She was unable to read
what was on the English cans of food that were

now piled high on the table in the tiny, cluttered kitchen, which was little more than a shed attached to the house.

"We've brought dog food for your dogs," Donald told Ion in bad French.

"For the dogs?" asked Ion in equally bad French.

"Yes, we feed our dogs in England. We don't shut them out at night. We take them for walks and out in the car and they live in the house with us," Donald said. It was something he had been wanting to say for a long time.

"Our dogs are just dogs," said Ion. "We let them out at night to kill things, to feed themselves. It's easier that way."

His French wasn't very good, and Donald only partly understood it, but what he did understand made him very angry. Then his father, who had been listening, called from the front of the van in English, "What do you expect, Donald? If you have nothing to eat yourselves? Be reasonable." And Donald thought of his mother, who adored all animals, dogs most of all. It was she who had packed the food for the dogs, saying as she did so that she preferred dogs to humans. It had seemed reasonable then, but now Donald wondered whether she was right, for the yard dogs were so savage that only Ion dared to stroke them. And though they would lick his hands, they snarled at everyone else.

Uncle Fanel and Ion's father had unloaded the medicines, syringes, powdered milk, and all the other things Uncle Fanel had brought for the hospital. Staff stepped forward to shake Uncle Fanel by the hand. Sad, somber faces were smiling now. Ion could see that his uncle's visit had filled them with hope, and he longed to see them all happy. The sun had come out. Grandmother was going to recover. The medicine would save her. It was another kind of miracle, no one could deny it. And Ion believed in miracles.

As they traveled home Uncle Fanel and Ion's father laughed together in the front of the van. Grandmother was going to be all right, they said. And they'd heard what the doctor said, "She's as strong as an ox."

Clean and well-dressed, Donald was wishing himself back in England, where most people would be smiling and the shops stocked full of food. When they reached home again, Donald went ahead into the house and then rushed out again shouting, "Ion, where are you? Come inside. Your mother is cooking dog food for lunch!"

Ion didn't understand what he was saying, so he fetched his father, who tipped the dog food outside in the yard while Ion's mother cried, "But it was good meat."

Ion felt overcome by shame, but rushed to his mother just the same, crying out in his own tongue, "It's not her fault. How could she know?"

So the meal was late, and Uncle Fanel impatient. The food he had brought was in the cellar now, guarded night and day by the yard dogs. Everyone in the village had received food and a bag of clothes. The van was empty. Then Uncle

Fanel ordered a banquet for the next day. "I must be back in England in two days, my job demands it," he said.

It would be cold on the veranda, but there was nowhere else to hold the banquet. A Gypsy fiddler was hired for the next day, and clothes that had not been worn for several years were brought out and aired. The only blot would be Grandma's absence, for she was usually the life and soul of a party. It was decided that Mr. Ditescu should be the guest of honor. The biggest argument was whether Stefan should be invited.

"Yes," said Uncle Fanel.

"No," said Ion's father.

In the end Mr. Ditescu was asked for his opinion. After some thought he announced, "Ask him but don't give him a present, for this might never have happened but for his telephone call to England, which was surely the act of a true friend. Because of this we must not leave him out. Besides, who knows what power he might hold in the future; such a man will never stay long at the bottom of a heap, you can be sure of that."

And so it was settled. Then Uncle Fanel wanted chickens killed for the banquet, but when he caught one and realized how thin it was, he changed his mind abruptly. The whole day everyone was rushing hither and thither. Fortunately Ion's mother seemed to have regained her strength; she did her best to prepare the foreign food brought by Uncle Fanel to suit all tastes, adding pepper and herbs and lashings of wine. Wine glasses and cutlery were borrowed. The old house hadn't known such activity for a long time.

Ion listened to the radio his father had borrowed. The revolution was progressing; new laws were already being passed. Work had stopped on the President's palace while the new government decided what should be done with such a place. The President had been buried in a secret, unmarked grave. Ion felt as though he was living inside a history book.

Donald had gone for a walk and was trying to

come to terms with what he was seeing. He couldn't help comparing the shops overflowing at home with the dreadful poverty all around him. He had visited the village before, but in the summer, and then there had been enough food for everyone. Now there was nothing. Since then the whole atmosphere had changed so much that it was hardly the same place. And the changes were for the worse, for while he had grown three inches, Ion had remained the same size and his arms had become more bent and his hands more callused. In a way Donald wished that he had never come, for now he felt as though he was actually living a nightmare.

When he returned to the house, a long table had been set up on the veranda and covered with a handworked embroidered cloth. Fresh bread had been brought by a peasant woman. Soup was bubbling on the stove in the kitchen. Ion had washed and smoothed down his hair and was wearing secondhand English clothes (which Donald recognized as once his), held together by a massive, hand-embroidered belt.

So gradually the scene was set for an evening none of them would ever forget. The fiddler arrived and was given food and wine. Stefan arrived bearing bananas and oranges, though where he got them from no one was prepared to ask. Grandma would not be sitting at the head of the table as she had so often in the past, but otherwise everything appeared perfect.

11

My Country Right or Wrong

So THE PEOPLE gathered, appearing through the approaching darkness, bringing all they had as gifts—a handworked mat, pickled walnuts in a jar, sickly sweets. Mr. Ditescu brought a precious bottle of brandy that had lain in his cellar for years awaiting such an occasion. Others brought dusty prunes, and one a piece of salted pork. Precious things were brought too. A silver locket for Ion's mother, a Swiss knife for Ion that had everything on it—a corkscrew, can opener, two blades, even a blade for picking stones from a horse's hoof. Donald was given an antique gun, which he would treasure all his life; Uncle Fanel a bottle of wine dated 1966. Soon the light was faint on the veranda, but the white snow all around added light. Every single person asked after Grandma, Ion noticed that. And they left her seat empty at the head of the table, none wishing to take her place, lest it should be a bad omen. There had never been such a gathering before. Long before the food appeared, toasts were drunk—to Grandma, to Uncle Fanel and his handsome son, to the revolution, which they were all still afraid to believe had really happened, and to Ion's parents, who had returned after so long, like lost people to claim their inheritance.

Ion was kept busy filling glasses, fetching more plates, cushions for the old to put behind their backs. Mr. Ditescu did not usually attend such gatherings; to have him there was a particular honor. Uncle Fanel begged him to sit in Grandma's chair, but he too refused, saying that no one should take the old lady's place, not while she was alive. And everyone ate the strange English food, as they had not eaten so well for months. The fiddler played the old tunes; soon people left the veranda to dance in their boots in the snow, their faces suddenly red with the cold and the food, but most of all with the wine.

Then, as the coffee from England was brewed, Mr. Ditescu stood up and said, "This toast is to Ion, the bravest of us all, who at twelve years old braved the police and the soldiers and went to find his parents, who ignored the chaos and the gunfire and brought them back to us here. To Ion."

Everyone raised their glasses while Ion muttered, "It was nothing."

"And now we want his story, word for word, because it is all part of history and the revolution. Ion," said Mr. Ditescu.

They put him on a chair, where he stood up, staring at their homely faces—the people he had known all his life; and he told his story. He told them that he had asked Stefan to telephone Uncle Fanel. He told them about his visit to the headquarters and the colonel soon to be dead;

of Cristina and the trip to the capital; he told of the bathroom where the taps ran with hot water, and of the candles in the street, lit to remember the dead, flickering all day long, and every moment his voice grew stronger. He told them about the drunk who had left him alone in the mountains and of the wicked doctor, and of the prison where he had found his parents, and as he spoke his voice grew so much in strength that people cried, "What a speaker! He will go far, this one." He told them of the journey home and how marvelous it was to find that the village was still there, not bulldozed into the earth as he had feared. "And that is all," he finished. "But one day I want to go back and find Cristina," and his voice broke a little then, so that they knew he was half in love with her, and then they laughed and cheered and cried, "Bravo!"

And even Donald turned to him then to cry, "Bravo!" in French and "Well done!" in English. And so the only thing Ion was missing now was his grandmother. He wanted to tell her how it had been and that he still had the photograph and some of the money she had given him, because everything had been free.

Then Uncle Fanel stood up and said how pleased he was to be with them and how all the world was watching the revolution with excitement and admiration. He was rather drunk by this time on Mr. Ditescu's plum brandy and his words tumbled over each other, but everyone cheered just the same.

Then the fiddler started to play louder than ever and Ion could feel exhaustion blotting everything out, making the voices seem dim and far away, and slowly sleep took over. When he awakened twenty minutes later, his mother was clearing up and Donald was complaining about his bed. "The mattress is hard and full of straw, and feathers are coming out of the pillow," he said.

Ion's father replied, "When you've been in prison as long as I have, young man, you'll learn that such things are not important."

And then Donald was silent, but his face was scowling.

They left the washing up till the morning. The moon was faint and far away now and the cocks in the village were heralding another day.

"Your speech was first-class, Ion," Uncle Fanel said, smelling of brandy, and rumpling Ion's hair as he spoke. "You're the real hero."

But Ion didn't feel like a hero, for everything had been easier than he had expected. And there hadn't been time to feel really afraid. He thought that maybe wars were like that; you just went on doing your best, ignoring everything else. And if you were lucky you survived.

Donald had his bed, so Ion slept as he had the night before, on a quilt on the floor in the living room, which smelled of garlic, sweat, and plum brandy. And he knew that in three hours it would be time to milk the cow again and let out the geese and feed the few thin chickens that were left. Then he thought about Mr. Ditescu, who was grave and wise and seemed to be two people, one a fierce, unbending schoolmaster, the other a kind, elderly man. He thought, I would like to be as he is when I'm older; everyone respects him. And I still want to be an official in the government, just as I always have, and perhaps if you want things enough they really do come true.

He slept. And when he wakened again it was another day. He leaped up, crying, "I've overslept! What about the cow?"

But his mother had milked the cow long ago. "You looked so tired, we left you to sleep," she said, kissing him on the forehead. "Your father and Uncle Fanel have gone to see Grandma. Donald is still sleeping. And there must be a lot of bad heads this morning in the village and a lot of hangovers."

And she laughed; and, listening to her laughter, Ion felt happier than he had in years. "You mean I don't have to milk the cow anymore?" he asked.

"I didn't say that. But yes, not every morning. I shall be doing it from now on, and today your father fetches the other two cows from the cooperative farm and I shall milk them too, if they're still in milk that is. And in the spring we'll have calves again, and with the revolution in place, things must surely get better," she finished.

Ion remembered the last calf, which was taken away to the cooperative farm in spite of his grandmother's protests. He remembered that they had only been allowed half a bag of maize because they hadn't a man to work on the cooperative farm, and his grandmother's tears. And he knew now why Donald's face was so untouched—it was because he hadn't seen such things, had never known what it was like to go to the cellar and see it empty. He had never had to guard the grapes all day long through a hot summer, nor watch his grandmother dying because she wasn't allowed medicine or a doctor.

But now Uncle Fanel and his father were returning. He could hear their laughter outside, which must mean that his grandmother was better. He ran outside to greet them, waving his thin arms, waking Donald, who was longing to be home again, far away from tired, gray faces.

"She's doing fine," said Uncle Fanel. "She really is; even the doctor is astounded. She'll be back home in a day or two, you'll see."

"They're selling oranges in the town," said his father. "Everything is opening up. There are foreigners coming in all the time with food and clothes and medical supplies. Why, they are even in Augusta!"

"We must go, but we will be back," said Uncle Fanel. "I am sending airline tickets, as many as you want, in the spring. For Ion in particular, because now he can return when he likes, so it needn't be forever." Uncle Fanel put his arm around Ion's shoulders. "Bring your grandmother too, Ion, if she's well enough to travel. Do you hear me?"

Ion felt as though he was choking, for now he could see it all—an enormous plane, his parents and his grandmother walking up the steps, sunlight on tarmac, cases laden with presents.

"We'll fatten you up. We want you for months, not weeks, Ion," his uncle said. "We want you to return fat and well, much taller and speaking English; with strong, straight arms. And if you decide to stay with us forever, you can. I'll see to that. I can even get you English nationality in time, Ion. That's a promise."

"Are you sure, Dad?" asked Donald, up and dressed now. "And would he fit in?"

"Of course, he would fit in," yelled Uncle Fanel. "Look at me! I fit in, don't I?"

"Only just. And he's different; they all are. If this place was England it would be different too, wouldn't it? We would have got rid of the President years ago. We would have had him removed."

"Shut up," shouted Uncle Fanel.

"I've missed Christmas because of this. You said there would be celebrations, Dad. Where are they?" demanded Donald.

Uncle Fanel translated what he said and then laughed loudly.

"Christmas has been forbidden to us for many years," replied Ion's father quietly. "Wait for New Year's, Donald; we'll celebrate that as best we can. As for resisting, maybe England has never been occupied as we have by the Romans, the Turks, Germans, Russians. And we've never had an empire."

And he wiped tears from his cheeks as he spoke, while Ion yelled, "I hate you, Donald. You're spoiled. You don't know what work is. You're just a spoiled poodle dog. You couldn't fight anyone. Why, you can't even sleep on a straw mattress without complaining." And then suddenly they were outside fighting in the snow. Uncle Fanel pulled them apart.

"How could you, when Donald has been so kind to you?" asked Ion's father. "Where are your manners, Ion? And, Donald, I must tell you that dictatorships are not toppled in a day. Read your history books. I have learned a lot in prison. I had time to think there, something I never had time for before. In a poor country anything can happen. And because you want to, you believe in promises that one day quite soon, things will be better."

Boosted by his father's support, Ion shouted, "But one day we will be strong, you'll see. And I don't want to be fattened up, Uncle Fanel. I'm fat enough, and how my arms are is my business. Okay? And I don't want to be English either. I love my country, okay?"

His parents looked shocked. "After such kindness," cried his mother, kissing Uncle Fanel's hand.

"He doesn't know what he says," added his father, and Ion despised them for being so humble.

"It was nothing. Boys will be boys and I like one with spirit," replied Uncle Fanel, laughing. "Think no more of it. And what he said was largely true and I am not offended. Besides, Donald didn't understand a word he said. He just caught the gist of it."

Donald got into the van. "He's so English. He

doesn't like to be kissed and embraced, or only by his girlfriend," explained Uncle Fanel. "He is so like his mother, it is unbelievable."

"We understand," replied Ion's father.

They were leaving now. "Donald's presents are awaiting him under the Christmas tree, so many things. I don't know right from wrong these days," said Uncle Fanel wearily, embracing Ion's parents. "We have so much and you have so little. It's a topsy-turvy world."

"Don't think of it." Ion's mother looked exhausted; she would be exhausted for a long time to come. "We will always be indebted to you, Fanel. We'll never forget," she said.

"And remember, Ion, whether the others come to England or not, you're expected. Forgive Donald for being as he is; he's in love and didn't want to tear himself away. I made him come. It was a mistake, but it may have done him some good, who knows?" said Uncle Fanel. And Ion, who would have liked to be in love himself, could think of nothing to say.

So Uncle Fanel got into his van, and tooting on the horn, left on his long journey back to England, and as he disappeared another car appeared, old and dirty, weaving its way through the potholes in the road.

"Whoever are they? They're waving to you, Ion," his mother cried.

The man inside had stubble on his cheeks and receding hair; his face was lean, his complexion the color of putty. And beside him sat Cristina, waving and laughing, her fair hair free, a gun no longer slung across her shoulder. Another minute and she was standing in the road crying, "So this is where you live, Ion. This is my husband. He has come back from the dead. What about your parents? Did you find them?"

"Here, both here. We're all together again," Ion answered, swallowing tears of excitement and joy. "But it was a close thing."

Cristina shook his parents by the hand, western style. "And this is Hans, my husband. It has been ten years since we were together and now it seems unbelievable. This is the third village we've visited looking for you, Ion. I had to know you were all right," she said.

Ion's father invited them inside, then sat discussing prison with Hans while Cristina said, "Our next child will be called Ion, if it's a boy. You have a very brave son, Mrs. Radu." And no one knew how to reply, least of all Ion.

His mother plied the guests with food and drink while Cristina told them about her life, how her grandparents had been rich and then, when everything had been taken from them, had sent her to be educated in France. She told them about her marriage and the paper she and Hans had printed that had criticized the government and sent him to prison for ten years. Then, weeping, she told them about the death of her son. "But now we will try again," she said. "We will have a new family, won't we, Hans?"

He nodded in agreement.

And then Ion told the story of his search all

over again, and when he had finished, Cristina said, "I hope that wicked doctor is never allowed to practice again."

"So do I. But now it is time to go," Hans said. And then Ion kissed Cristina's hand and so did his father. Cristina kissed Ion's mother on the cheek, saying that they must keep in touch and that since Hans's parents lived in Augusta, it would be easy. And so for the second time that day Ion and his parents stood outside waving good-bye.

When the car had completely disappeared, his mother turned to Ion and said, "As long as we live we will never forget what you have been through for us, Ion."

And his father added, "I would rather have you around than young Donald any day. He can't even milk a cow. He likes to keep his hands clean, that's what it is."

Ion looked at his own lined hands and thought, they're like old friends. They'll never let me down. But he still wished they were different. Then he looked at his parents and saw the gaunt beauty of his mother and the strength in his father's worn face, and he thought: I've been on a long search, but it's been worth it a thousand times over. And now, in Ion's imagination, he saw his grandmother coming home, cows returning from the cooperative farm, the cellar full of food, the grapes ripening in the vineyard. Another harvest, another grape-picking, the cows growing fat on summer grass, calves and piglets, chicks and goslings. With help from Mr. Ditescu, he would go to college. He would no longer be responsible for his grandmother but free to go out into the world to seek his fortune. But however far he went, he knew he would always return to the village. His mother touched his cheek. "Stop daydreaming and come inside. Your father's lit the stove," she said.

He followed her in and so, for the first time in years, he sat with his parents. And now Ion couldn't stop talking. "Did I tell you about the President? I saw him, Mother. He was just an ordinary person in rather shabby clothes,

Father, and no one could hear him when he spoke. He looked like anyone." And then Ion laughed as he had not in years, the tears rolling down his cheeks, and all the horror of the revolution and the fear of his search were distant now, like something viewed from afar. All that mattered now was that his parents were with him at last, sitting around the stove—home.